Yeti and the Great TREK

Trekking across South Africa on a rollicking, hilarious reading-safari

Marius Oelschig

Yeti and the Great TREK

ISBN 978-0-9948479-5-9

Published as a print-on-demand book
through CreateSpace, an Amazon company,

Printed in the United States of America

Author's photo courtesy of The Western Wheel,
Okotoks AB

Cover design: Dan Huckle, Okotoks AB
(danhuckle.com)

First printing, May 2018

Also by Marius Oelschig

Wally – A story about what happened *after* Christmas.

Two Warriors – Dealing with bullies at school.

Jak of the Bushveld – A glimpse into the life of a boy growing up on a farm in the Bushveld of South Africa

Jessi – The everyday adventures of a nature-loving South African girl

Scrap – The adventures of an extraordinary South African dog

The Wishing Stone – A children's historical novel about life in gold-rush South Africa

Storm Clouds over Egoli – A children's historical novel about life in the Transvaal – just before the Boer War

The above books, for children of all ages, are available as Kindle e-books or as print-on-demand books through Amazon

This book is dedicated to my grand-children

Zasha and Zayden Rabie

They are proud Canadians, but
I want them to be proud of South Africa
too. May you, Kiewiet and Patrys, enjoy reading
this book as much as I enjoyed writing it for you.

1

The Contestants

Have you ever heard of the Great Trek? Well, this TREK is a very special event that takes place in the Republic of South Africa every once in a while. The word TREK is an abbreviation and stems from its full title or description – the **T**rans **R**epublic **E**xpedition for **K**ids. When Louis the Lion King, the King of the beasts, feels like it (which is not very often) he invites four South African children, and their special guests, to race across the Republic of South Africa. That is probably where all the modern-day TV reality shows got the idea.

There is no prize. The prize is just the fun of taking part in the race. The race starts at the top of Table Mountain, right at the southern tip of South Africa, and it ends way up in the north, on a farm called

"Last Penny", where the Limpopo River forms the border between South Africa and Zimbabwe.

One morning it dawned on Louis that he would soon celebrate his 40th birthday. The idea of getting so old made him gloomy, so he decided to brighten things up by having another Great TREK. He sent out invitations to apply for participation in the TREK in the press and on TV. For many months he received and read applications from young boys and girls from all over South Africa. Finally he decided on the four lucky contestants. They were:

- ✓ Bobby Breen from Bloemfontein
- ✓ Kosie Koekemoer from Cradock
- ✓ Dorothy Dunbar from Durban and,
- ✓ John Andrew Kingston, also known as JAK of the Bushveld.

The Lion King wrote letters to the four children explaining the rules of the Race. Each child would also be allowed to invite a small team of friends from a foreign country to accompany them during the race. The idea was to encourage visitors to come to South Africa, then for them to return home and tell all their friends and family about the wonderful place South Africa really is.

Bobby Breen wanted to invite the King of England. This very important gentleman decided to send Humpty Dumpty in his place and, to keep him company, he also sent all the King's horses and all the King's men. If anything happened to Humpty Dumpty, surely ***they*** would be able to put him back together again?

Kosie Koekemoer, who was crazy about racing cars, invited Sterling Mustard, the famous American NASCAR racing driver (with his newest, fastest racing car), and his Scottish mechanic Mac, to be his guests.

Dorothy Dunbar invited Noddy and Big Ears from Tow Town in England to be her guests and to assist her during the race.

Jak thought about the problem for a while. He discussed the matter with his trusty companion Rusty, his Fox Terrier dog. They finally invited Yeti, the Abominable Snowman and Ruler of Shangri-La, to be Jak's guest. They also invited Yeti to bring a friend, any friend … if he had a friend.

As you may know, Yeti lives in the foothills of the Himalayan Mountains in the Kingdom of Shangri-La – but you knew that, didn't you? The Kingdom of Herenthere was the next-door kingdom ruled by Queen Lilywhite, his neighbour. Queen Lilywhite, however, had a top secret secret. She was, in fact, the wicked witch Nastimania. When Queen Lilywhite (Nastimania) heard that Yeti was going to South Africa, she was jealous. When she was jealous she was horrid! She had never been to Africa herself, but knew that there were all manner of wild animals there. With any luck, Yeti would be eaten by a lion or a crocodile or trampled by an elephant or a rhinoceros while on his visit. Perhaps she could even encourage that to happen, she thought. She would then take over the Kingdom of Shangri-La and become the Queen of Two-Kingdoms. She wanted that more than anything in the world.

So, one dark and stormy night, Queen Lilywhite saddled her broom and paid a quick visit to Toy Town, in England. While Noddy and Big Ears were having their tea, she waved her magic wand and chanted the magic password, turning them into two spiders sitting on the table. At midnight the following day, they were "back to normal" again, but had forgotten all about their invitation to visit South Africa.

Back in her "kingdom", Nastimania wrote a letter to Dorothy Dunbar in Durban telling her that Noddy and Big Ears were "indisposed" and were not able to travel to South Africa, but that Queen Lilywhite and her son, Prince Bandilegs, would be very pleased to take their place.

Nastimania did not have a son. She was far too selfish to share anything with anyone. So, when necessary, she would turn her pet frog Fungus into the charming and handsome Prince Bandilegs. It was the first devious plot in what was to become a most interesting TREK.

The happiest guest of all was Yeti, also known as the Abominable Snowman or **Big Foot**. Yeti was a very shy creature. He was also HUGE – something in the order of a snowy-white giant monster-ogre. He always wore a thick, white, fluffy coat knitted for him by his mum from the softest, warmest, whitest mountain-goat wool. Because of his size, everyone was scared of him, so he only went out in blizzards, when no one could see him. He often helped mountain-climbers in trouble on the mountains, so some people had seen him, but never clearly. All they ever found were his footprints in the snow – hence his nick-name, **Big Foot**.

Yeti had no brothers, only four sisters; Beti, Heti, Leti and Neti. Although Yeti was the Ruler (or King) of Shangri-La, his little sisters (all of them over seven feet tall) bossed him around terribly. His best friend was Dodgy, a dour and smelly old mountain-goat. Dodgy got this name when he applied for the job of Regimental Mascot for a British regiment serving in India. When he went for the interview, he was turned down; the Regimental Sergeant-Major, or RSM, declaring that he "smelt a bit dodgy". The name stuck.

So, Yeti was really looking forward to seeing new sights, making new friends and, most of all, getting away from his four "little" sisters.

2

Ready, Steady, TREK.

Eventually everyone arrived in Cape Town. Humpty Dumpty, with all the King's Horses and all the King's Men, arrived by sailing ship. There were so many horses and so many riders and so many grooms and so much fodder and so many soldiers that it took seven ships to bring them all from England.

Sterling Mustard, his racing car, Mac the mechanic and the transporter-truck arrived in a steamship from America, where they had been racing in the Indy 500. The only thing they needed when they arrived in Cape Town was gas.

"Ons hettie gas by hierrie fillien staysun," an attendant told them in the strange dialect of the Cape Province (we don't have "gas" at this filling station). It took some time before someone told Sterling Mustard and Mac that in South Africa they would have to ask for **petrol** and not gas, the American abbreviation for gasoline.

Nastimania, presenting herself as Queen Lilywhite from the Kingdom of Herenthere, arrived at midnight on her broom, when no one could see her. She brought everything that she needed in a shoebox; her magic wand, Fungus the frog, five white mice and a bunch of fleas. Oh yes, there were also three grasshoppers in her shoebox. They were really three nasty, short, fat, ugly trolls called Greaseball, Meatball and Furball. The three trolls accompanied her wherever she went. Every wicked witch needs nasty helpers for her nasty business, you see. Because there was no place for them on her broom, Nastimania travelled with the three trolls disguised as grasshoppers in her shoebox instead.

When a magic wand comes from the factory, it comes with a special password. This is an essential safety feature. Without this password, a magic wand is useless. So, if someone finds a magic wand but they don't have the password, they can do no harm. And a password without a magic wand is like a bicycle without wheels … or a chocolate teapot – it doesn't work! Nastimania was becoming quite forgetful, so she carried her magic password written on a piece of paper, hidden under her foot in her shoe. The password for her magic wand was **RAMBAKAZAM!** Without it, all her spells were useless.

Yeti the Abominable Snowman and Dodgy the goat arrived by boat. Not a sailing boat, or a motorboat, or a ferry, or a yacht. They arrived by rowing boat, which Yeti rowed across the ocean all by himself … in a total of 24 hours and thirteen minutes, or fourteen minutes for the superstitious.

Bobby Breen, Kosie Koekemoer, Dorothy Dunbar and Jak met their guests at the Town Hall. The Mayor of Cape Town welcomed all the visitors in the crowded Town Hall – what with all the King's horses and all the King's men. He then told the four teams that they needed to choose their team colours.

"Royal blue and gold," said Humpty Dumpty in a very royal voice. "Those are the King's colours, and everyone is already dressed in those colours."

"Red and yellow," said Sterling Mustard. "My racing colours in South Africa will be red and yellow."

"White and pink and baby-blue with a splash of silver and a touch of gold," said Queen Lilywhite. Dorothy Dunbar groaned, the Mayor rolled his eyes, but the tailors, who thought they would get the job of fitting out the team in these magnificent colours, smiled broadly.

Jak and Yeti looked at each another and, with a big grin on their face and in one voice said, "White.

Himalayan White with a touch of cream and a pinch of beige. Oh yes … and khaki for Jak."

Queen Lilywhite gave them both an ugly look.

Bright and early the next morning, everyone assembled on the square in front of the Castle in Cape Town. They all looked quite splendid in their new racing colours, although Yeti and Jak looked decidedly "milky" compared to the other teams. All the citizens of Cape Town were in a festive mood, everyone except the tailors who, for some strange reason, had not been given any work to do by Dorothy Dunbar and Queen Lilywhite.

"Is everyone here?" asked the Mayor in his important mayor's voice. He was looking at Dorothy Dunbar and Queen Lilywhite. "Where is the rest of your team? Where is your transport? Where is Prince Bandilegs?"

Nastimania had, as usual, forgotten about everyone else, thinking only of herself.

"One moment, Lord Mayor," she said and disappeared around a corner into a deserted Cape Town alley.

Quickly she took out her shoebox, removed her magic wand, Fungus the frog and the five white mice and the three grasshoppers. She then took a quick peek at the bit of paper in her shoe.

"**RAMBAKAZAM!**" she said, with a flick of her wand.

POOF! The shoebox became a beautiful royal coach, four white mice became four magnificent white horses, the fifth mouse turned into a beautiful white stallion for the Prince and Fungus had turned into the handsome and charming Prince Bandilegs. Greaseball, Meatball and Furball were the royal pageboys that carried the Queen's long train (she loved trains) ... and her shoebox.

"Here we are, Lord Mayor," trilled Nastimania in her pleasant queen's voice. "All present and raring to go!"

"There are far too many people for us all to go to the top of Table Mountain for the start of the TREK," said the Mayor. "Each boy will be allowed to take one member of his team."

Well, it took the rest of the day to get Humpty Dumpty and Sterling Mustard's car to the top of Table Mountain. It would take just as much time to get them down again and that meant that they would delay their team at the start of the race. Kosie Koekemoer and Bobby Breen were already regretting their choice of guests to participate in the Great TREK.

By late afternoon everyone was assembled on top of Table Mountain. It was a lovely warm afternoon and the view over Cape Town and Table Bay was magnificent. The mayor looked at the four children and their guests, nodded his head and then, holding a silk handkerchief, lifted his hand into the air.

"Ready, steady, TREK," he cried, dropping his hand.

Rockets and other fireworks shot up into the sky. They burst overhead with load bangs, leaving trails of tiny red and yellow stars showering down over the city. The people of Cape Town clapped their hands and cheered, all the pigeons in the city rose up and flew off in fright and all the dogs started barking.

The Great TREK was under way.

3

The Fruit of the Vine

Stellenbosch! Ah, Stellenbosch! (Get your Mom or Dad to show you a map of South Africa. Now get them to show you where Stellenbosch is. Better still, find it on Google Earth). This beautiful town at the foot of the Helshoogte Pass is world famous for its vineyards. Do you know what fruit grows in a vineyard? Yup, that's right – grapes. And what are grapes used for? Well, we eat grapes, sure, but grapes are normally pressed and most of the juice is used in the making of wine. So, Stellenbosch is really world famous for its world famous wine.

When the wine farmers of Stellenbosch heard that the Great TREK would be passing through their town, they immediately organised a huge big party. They were not interested in the Great TREK, they just wanted everyone to taste their world famous wine. While Sterling Mustard wanted to get on with the race and Yeti wanted to see the country and the wild animals, all the other competitors (especially Humpty Dumpty and his entourage) were only too happy to stop for a party. The four children, Kosie and Dorothy and Bobby and Jak, got together and agreed that perhaps it would be a good idea to stop over in Stellenbosch for the night.

Humpty Dumpty and Queen Lilywhite were overjoyed. Humpty was feeling a little sick from being jolted around on the back of a cart and needed the rest ... and time to patch up the first fine cracks in his shell – with vinegar and brown paper. Queen Lilywhite was a bit of a party animal. After all, besides doing the odd bit of nasty business as Nastimania, the Queen of Herenthere did little more than attend balls and parties and shows and concerts. And Queen Lilywhite **did** enjoy a good glass of wine.

Now, drinking a glass of wine is fine. But people who drink *too much* wine become noisy, foolish and reckless. They use bad language, they fight, they fall around, they break things and generally make a nuisance of themselves. The next morning they all pay dearly for their bad behaviour – they feel horribly, awfully sick! They have dreadful headaches, they feel nauseous, they can't eat and they can't think clearly. In Stellenbosch they call this the *"wingerdgriep"*. In

Afrikaans it is known as a *"babbalas"*. Elsewhere in the world this is called a *"hangover"*. I prefer the Stellenbosch description, which means *"vineyard influenza."*

The morning after the party, even before the cock had crowed in Stellenbosch, the Red 'n Yellow team of Kosie Koekemoer and Sterling Mustard was up and off like a flash. With instructions to Mac to meet them in Matjiesfontein (have another look at the map) they raced out of town in a cloud of dust.

By the time the sun came up, Yeti and Dodgy and Jak were at the top of Helshoogte Pass overlooking the valley. They were also heading for Matjiesfontein, with Jak sitting comfortably on Yeti's shoulders and Dodgy trotting along behind, grumbling about having to get up so early in the morning.

Just outside Stellenbosch, in the camp set up for Humpty Dumpty and his entourage (ask Mom what this word means), there was total confusion. Bobby Breen was stamping his feet in frustration. He wanted to get on with the TREK, but all the King's horses had to be watered, fed, groomed and saddled. All the King's men had to wash and shave and have their breakfast. Humpty Dumpty had to be carefully placed in a special cart filled with new straw and soft pillows so that he would not crack his shell any further. It would be some hours before everyone was ready to move out on the next leg of the TREK.

But if there was confusion in Bobby Breen's camp, there was total chaos in the hotel where the Pink 'n Blues were staying. After about ten minutes of banging on Queen Lilywhite's hotel room door, Dorothy Dunbar managed to wake her up. The poor old witch (sorry, Queen) was suffering from a serious bout of *"vineyard influenza."* The world famous wine was giving her a world famous headache.

"Where am I?" she whispered as she peered around through bleary, unfocused, bloodshot eyes. "What happened?" she asked as she gingerly held her hand to a head that felt like a hollow ball of steel with a crazy woodpecker inside, trying to peck his way out.

"Get moving, Your Majesty," yelled Dorothy, banging even more loudly on the locked door. "It's already ten o'clock and we're way behind in the race. Where is Prince Bandilegs? Where is our coach? Where are the horses?"

Now, before we proceed, some explanation is required. Remember Nastimania's magic wand? Good! Now this magic wand was neither the best nor the most expensive wand available on the market. If it were a motorcar, the wand was certainly not a Porche, nor a Rolls Royce, not even a Cadillac. It was more like an old rusty beaten-up second-hand World War II Army truck. Consequently (pass the dictionary, please) the spells that were cast using this magic wand were also on the "cheap and shabby" side. Nastimania's spells would only last until the stroke of midnight, after which everything would revert back to what it was before. This is often very convenient – just ask Noddy and Big Ears, but can also be very **in**convenient – just ask Cinderella. So Queen Lilywhite, in her baggy Nastimania pyjamas and with a thumping headache, had Prince Bandilegs, the pageboys, the coach and all the horses in a shoebox under her bed.

Bang! Bang! **Bang!** It was Dorothy Dunbar at the door again.

"I'm almost ready," said Queen Lilywhite in a hoarse and shaky voice. "Just give me a moment."

Grabbing the shoebox, she clambered (very unladylike) out of the window and fell down with a thud into the sandy courtyard below, sending up a small cloud of dust, She opened the box, removed the magic wand and Fungus, took out the five white mice and the three grasshoppers and laid them out on the cobbled driveway. She then made to remove her shoe to have a peek at her password. Oh my soul! She was standing there … barefoot. With her head pounding like a jackhammer, she tried to remember the password. She tried and she tried. She tried some more. Eventually, in sheer desperation and with a flick of the magic wand, she mumbled **"RAMBOKAZAMBO."** (Was that the correct password? Duh! Hello? Not even close!)

KADOEF! (It should have been **POOF!** ... right?)

The shoebox turned into a rusty old bucket. The five white mice turned into purple rabbits. Fungus the frog became a pot-bellied pig with green and yellow stripes and the grasshoppers turned into three smelly billy-goats that started chewing on Nastimania's pyjamas.

There was a loud groan in the courtyard and Nastimania was last seen clambering back through the window into her bedroom where she stayed for the rest of the day, refusing to open her door. Not even for lunch. Not even for a glass of world famous Stellenbosch wine.

4

Cruising through the Karoo

There was a huge cloud of dust hanging over the Karoo. There was no wind and the dust just hung there, causing everyone to sneeze and rub their eyes.

"Where is all this dust coming from?" asked a puzzled farmer, peering through the gloom at his dusty sheep.

The culprit was Sterling Mustard.

"There are too many cops and too many speed-traps and too many road-blocks on the highways," he told Kosie Koekemoer. "Back home, when I'm in a hurry, I take the back roads."

What Sterling did not know was that the back roads in South Africa are gravel roads. Driving on gravel roads makes a lot of dust. Especially when you drive really fast, the way Sterling was accustomed to driving.

"If we want to win this race we have to drive fast. Really fast!" said Sterling.

Kosie Koekemoer just smiled. He loved every minute of it.

Suddenly, while travelling at one hundred miles per hour, Sterling and Kosie heard a strange sound. It was very much like the sound of a bicycle bell. They heard it again. It ***was*** the sound of a bicycle bell. Kosie looked in the rear view mirror but all he could see was a huge cloud of dust. Then, out of the dust-cloud, came the figure of someone on a bicycle, pedalling furiously and madly ringing the bicycle bell. The figure pulled alongside the racing car. It was a policeman.

"Pull over!" the policeman shouted, pointing to the side of the road.

Sterling pulled over, very carefully, and Kosie got out of the car to face the law. The policeman parked his bike against a straggly thorn tree and spent about ten minutes slapping his short-pants uniform and his cap to remove the layers of dust. When he finally emerged from his own private dust-storm, he joined Kosie and Sterling with a huge smile on his dusty face.

"*Jislaaik, Meneer,* (Gee, Sir)" he said showing off his teeth that were brown from the dust. "This car of yours can really move."

"My name is Koos," said the policeman, introducing himself. "Constable Koos van der Merwe of the S A P S, the South African Police Service. I was just patrolling these hillocks around here, checking up on the *veediefstal* (stock-theft), when I saw you motoring past a little faster than a local donkey cart. I am afraid that you are under arrest for breaking the speed limit. Please follow me to the *polisiekantoor* (police station) in Beaufort-Wes where I shall file my report."

With that the policeman walked over to his bike, mounted it and sedately rode off in the direction of Beaufort-Wes, somewhere over the horizon. Sterling Mustard and Kosie followed the policeman's bicycle … just as sedately.

At that very moment Yeti, Jak and Dodgy were just moving through the little town of Laingsburg.

"When are we going to see some of your famous wild animals?" asked Yeti. "We've been travelling for two days now and all I've seen is Dodgy."

"Have you seen an ostrich before?" asked Jak, pointing in the direction of the long-legged bird he had spotted in a field by the side of the road.

"Can we go over and have a closer look?" pleaded Yeti. "Can we? Can we?"

Without waiting for an answer, Yeti stepped over the fence and walked in the direction of the ostrich. The ostrich did what ostriches normally do — it ran away. Now, I suppose you know that the ostrich is the fastest bird in the world, right? With its long legs, an ostrich can out-run a horse. Well this ostrich, which was renowned in the district for its speed, found that it could not out-run Yeti. Soon the two of them were bounding neck-and-neck across the wide-open Karoo. Now, when an ostrich runs it makes very little dust, but when Yeti runs he makes a huge cloud of dust. It must be those huge, big, flat feet pounding the dry veld with such tremendous force. Anyway, the ostrich and Yeti were making a huge cloud of dust.

Jak was sitting with his back to a milestone watching Yeti on safari … viewing the game in his own peculiar way. As he sat watching, Jak saw a figure approaching on a bicycle. Soon a policeman in a short-pants uniform joined him.

"Good day, *Boetie* (young man)," said the policeman politely. "My name is Piet. Constable Piet van der Merwe of the S A P S. We've had some strange reports about mysterious dust-clouds around here today".

As Jak and Piet watched, Yeti completed his inspection of the ostrich, turned around and came dashing back to the road leaving a dense trail of dust behind.

"*Jislaaik, Meneer* (Gee, Sir)," said Constable Piet, looking up at the white giant. "You're big and you're fast. And I just love your track-suit. Do you play rugby for the Springboks?"

Jak then told the policeman all about Yeti and Dodgy and explained that they were his guests in South Africa for the Great TREK.

"Ja well no fine," said Piet. "Welcome to South Africa, but I'm afraid that I can't let you rush around the countryside looking at all the animals and making so much dust."

"How are we going to solve the problem?" asked Jak. "Yeti wants to see the animals, but we're also in a race up to the Limpopo River."

"I'll tell you what," said the friendly policeman. "I come from Merweville, which is the dead centre (couldn't be deader) of the Great Karoo. (Get your Dad to show you where this is on a Google Earth map). Let's announce to everyone in the Karoo that Yeti is visiting Merweville tomorrow. We'll invite all the people and all the animals to come and meet him."

And that is what they did. The next day, in Merweville, the animals came from all over the Karoo to meet Yeti, the Ruler of the Kingdom of Shangri-La. There were springbokkies, bontebokke, meercats, honey badgers, jakkalse, tortoises, gemsbokke, blesbokke, kudus, impalas, elande, likkewane (leguans), geitjies (lizards), quaggas and hundreds of different types of birds. By the way, a quagga is really a zebra except that a quagga only has stripes on its head, neck and shoulders. The rear end of a quagga is brown, like a donkey.

"I thought that you had disappeared from the Earth," said Yeti to a really fine-looking quagga stallion.

"No way," said the quagga with a twinkle in his eye. "We just hide away in the dense growth of the valleys here in the Karoo. We're still very much around, but we just don't like tourists and hunters. In our case, it does ***not*** pay to advertise."

And still the crowds came to Merweville. There were farmers and farmers wives. There were schoolchildren and teachers, tractor drivers, farm labourers, bankers, mechanics, postmen and all kinds of other people; all having travelled from miles around to meet Yeti.

"If this goes on for much longer we'll never win the race," grumbled Dodgy as a fat little boy chewing on a stick of biltong poked him in his tummy. "But at least we won't get arrested for kicking up too much dust."

That evening, just after sunset, Yeti strapped Dodgy to his back, lifted Jak onto his shoulders and loped off into the night in a northerly direction, leaving a long trail of thick, powdery dust in his wake.

5

Flashing through the Free State

The Free State is as flat as your hand. Well, your hand is not really flat, is it? If you look carefully you will see dips and bumps and lines and folds on your hand. Go on, have a look! The Free State looks a lot like that, but on a far grander scale. But the Free State is still very flat. Not many trees either. But lots of grass. And lots of sheep.

Yeti was bored. "I'm tired of looking at this flat country," he grumbled as he dragged his weary feet across the dry, stony ground. "I'm tired of looking at sheep all day and I'm tired of carrying the two of you all over South Africa."

Sitting high up on Yeti's shoulders Jak realised that he had to do something or Yeti would have nothing but bad things to say about South Africa when he returned to the Kingdom of Shangri-La.

"Let's build a soapbox car," said Jak in his "I'm-so-clever-and-so-keen" voice. "We'll build a soapbox car, then Dodgy will help me push you all the way to Bloemfontein."

Dodgy was about to protest when Yeti excitedly agreed. "That's a great idea, Jak. No one has ever pushed me around in a soapbox car before. It'll be just great."

So they built a soapbox car. Have you ever built a soapbox car? It isn't easy. All the soapboxes that they tried were no good. Yeti broke them all the moment he sat down in them. Finally, in an abandoned farm shed, they came across a huge old wooden wool-crate that was strong enough.

The next problem was in finding suitable wheels. They tried shopping-trolley wheels. They tried roller-skate wheels. They tried baby-pram wheels. They tried bicycle wheels. All the wheels that they tried broke the moment Yeti sat down on the car. They eventually solved the problem by using four wagon wheels that they found on the carcass of an old rotting ox-wagon that was probably used by the Voortrekkers during the *real* Great Trek.

When the "soapbox car" was finally completed it was big

and strong and … really heavy. So heavy, in fact, that Jak and Dodgy just couldn't push it.

"I knew it, I knew it," complained Yeti. "We've built a soapbox car so that I can push the two of you around in it."

Jak was disappointed. He so badly wanted to have Yeti enjoy his time in South Africa. Jak and Yeti and Dodgy sat by the side of the road next to their huge, big, useless soapbox car. They didn't say a word. They sat in silence in the long, slim shade of a windmill that was pumping nice cool water over Yeti's blistered feet and into a drinking trough where the sheep were standing in line waiting for a drink. Jak and Dodgy sat listening to the whirr of the windmill's blades as they watched the tumbleweeds blowing across the vast sea of grass.

"Eureka!" shouted Jak. "I have it! I have a wonderful idea! Look at the tumbleweeds. They're being blown along by the wind. The wind is turning the windmill that is pumping the water. It's always windy here in the Free State. Let's put a sail on the soapbox car and let the wind blow us all the way to Bloemfontein."

"You've got it! By Jove, you've got it!" cried Yeti as the three friends held hands and danced a merry jig around the lonely Free State windmill.

The sheep scattered – then turned and watched in amazement as the Great TREK travellers kicked up the dust around their drinking trough.

Fortunately they had built a really strong soapbox car to carry the bulky Yeti, so putting up a sail wasn't a major problem. They found an old burnt-out tent by the side of the road. It was probably used by the road-builders a long time ago, but it still had enough canvas for the sail. They then used a telephone pole for a mast, tied the sail to the mast and off they went.

On that first day everything went really well and the three adventurers covered a lot of ground in their sailing soapbox car. On the second day, however, there was a problem. A huge, big problem; there was too much wind.

The day started out calmly enough until suddenly, at around tea-time (that's at about ten o'clock in the morning in South Africa) Yeti couldn't steer the boat (sorry, car) anymore. The wind had filled the sail to capacity. It billowed out in front of the car like a circus tent. Suddenly they were racing across the ground, unable to stick to the road. With the old wagon-wheels groaning and creaking loudly, they bounded over the uneven ground, over anthills and koppies (rocky outcrops), through ploughed lands, sunflower fields and thorn bush, rushing along like some infernal machine created by a crazy scientist, leaving a long streamer of thick dust behind them.

Dodgy was at the bottom of the crate with his ears over his eyes and his hoofs over his ears. Jak was hanging on for dear life peering over the edge of the crate, dreading the crash that he was sure would come. All he could see was a blur of bush, koppies, cattle, farmhouses, telephone poles and wide-open spaces. Yeti was hanging on to the mast with one hand raised above his head like some drunken pirate Captain.

"Yee-haaaaaa," he cried joyfully into the wind. "This is better! This is the way to go! Yee-haaaaaaaaaa!"

At around sunset the wind dropped. The sky was pink and red and orange. This is caused by the rays of the sun reflecting off particles of dust in the atmosphere, and our three travellers had been responsible for several tons of dust particles in the atmosphere that day. As the sailing soapbox car came to a grinding, creaking halt the three weary passengers were joined by another dusty figure that appeared out of the gloom riding a bicycle.

"Jislaaik, Menere," (gee, gentlemen) he said as he parked his bike against the side of the soapbox car. "I've been riding in your dust for about six hours. Do you have some spare water in that box of yours?"

Jak gave the man a canteen of water. He took a long, slow swallow and then introduced himself.

"My name is Jannie. Constable Jannie van der Merwe of the S A P S. My *nefies* (cousins) from the Karoo warned me about you. They told me that you were kicking up a storm of dust down there."

"Oh no," said Jak. "Please don't tell me that you're going to arrest us for making dust in the Free State."

"No, Sir," said the policeman taking out his notebook. He slowly turned over page after page as he read his scribbled notes. "I'm going to arrest you for knocking down five *windpompe* (windmills), for breaking through about ninety-five *doringdrade* (barbed-wire fences), for frightening one thousand eight hundred sheep and for scattering Mrs van Deventer's chickens to the four winds. Then there is the little matter of breaking the speed limit in the Free State for about six hours non-stop, not to mention the destruction of the telephone lines to forty three farms, four towns and two villages – all in one day."

Yeti and Dodgy and Jak looked sadly at one another. It seemed that they would be held up again by clashing heads with the law.

"If you'll just follow me to Reddersburg, gentleman" said the policeman as he mounted his bicycle and headed off into the night, leading the way with his wavering, dim little bicycle lamp.

"I just knew that this soapbox car was built for me to push you two around in," grumbled Yeti as he put his shoulder to the wheel.

Jak and Dodgy jumped out of the soapbox and together the three friends pushed their contraption all the way to Reddersburg with *another* Constable van der Merwe as their personal police escort.

6

The Dam of Tears

Three very tired and footsore friends pushed an over-sized soapbox car into the car park of the police station in Reddersburg. Wearily, with their shoulders drooping, they followed Constable van der Merwe into the building where they were expecting to be locked up in a tiny cell. Instead, as they entered the building, they found a long table laden with food and cool drinks. But there was no one to be seen.

"SURPRISE!" A young man dressed in a soldier's uniform suddenly appeared through another door.

"Jak!" he said, "I've been waiting here for you since sunset. What has taken you so long?"

It was Jak's Uncle Eddie, his mom's brother. Eddie was a paratrooper, stationed in Bloemfontein.

Some farming friends had phoned to tell him about the runaway soapbox car and the confusion that it had created. After their escapades in the Karoo, which had been reported on the news all over South Africa, Eddie knew that Jak, Yeti and Dodgy were the culprits. Eddie made enquiries and it was not long before he learned that Jak and his friends were heading for Reddersburg. Not long after that Eddie was in the little Free State *dorpie* (town), waiting for Jak and his two friends from the Kingdom of Shangri-La.

Well, there was a grand reunion, as Jak had not seen his Uncle Eddie for several months. Yeti was also pleased to see Eddie. It meant that they would not be spending the night on a hard bed in a police cell. He was also **very** pleased to see all the delicious food that Eddie had brought. When Constable van der Merwe learned that Jak and his foreign friends were contestants in the Great TREK, he dismissed all the charges against them with a stern warning not to frighten farm animals and not to speed so recklessly across the plains of South Africa. He also asked them to leave their very strange soapbox car in front of the police station, as he was convinced that it would, one day, become an important tourist attraction.

After they had eaten, Eddie bundled the three soapbox car racers into his Army Land Rover and took them to his Regiment in Bloemfontein. There he found two empty beds for Jak and Yeti and a nice patch of lawn for Dodgy to sleep on.

"Get some rest," said Eddie the paratrooper, "tomorrow we're all going to jump from an aeroplane."

Eddie was a lieutenant in the Parachute Regiment. He and his soldiers were to participate in a field exercise, starting with a parachute jump on a small dropping zone just outside the military base called the *koeikamp* (that's a cow pasture in English). Eddie decided to smuggle Jak and his friends onto the plane and to also have them jump with his troops.

Yeti was soon a great favourite with the soldiers. He told them all about his Kingdom and about his adventures in South Africa. There was a lot of laughing when Yeti told his stories about game viewing in the Karoo and sailing across the Free State in a soapbox car. All the while the preparations were made for the exercise and before long everyone was loaded into the four-engined C-130 Hercules transport aircraft, ready for the jump.

Before they took off from the airfield, Yeti asked Eddie at what height they would be jumping from the aircraft.

"From six hundred feet above the ground," said Eddie loudly above the roar of the engines. Yeti had a funny look on his face, but didn't say a word.

Soon the paratroopers and our Great TREK friends were flying over Bloemfontein looking down at the people, the roads, houses, shops, schools, churches and playing fields. Dodgy couldn't see a thing. He had his ears over his eyes and his hoofs over his ears.

"OK, everyone," called Lieutenant Eddie, "we're getting closer. Get ready to jump."

All the soldiers stood up, one behind the other. A red light came on. The line moved towards the open door. A green light came on. One by one the soldiers appeared through the door of the aircraft and jumped.

People on the ground were watching as the paratroopers jumped from the aircraft. One by one the soldiers came out and a moment later a parachute would open up, hanging in the air like a small green umbrella. Soon there was a long string of green parachutes across the sky. Then the people saw a much smaller person jump from the aircraft, soon after to be suspended below a large parachute. It was Jak. Then they saw something with four legs fall out of the aircraft, also to be suspended below a parachute. It was Dodgy.

Then a very large, round person with a white furry coat and big feet jumped from the aircraft. No parachute opened behind him. The large, round body plummeted to the ground. With a loud **THUD** and a great ball of dust the body bounced back into the air like a rubber ball, twisting and turning and somersaulting like crazy. Then it hit the ground again, and bounced back into the air again. Bouncing and tumbling, leaving a long trail of thick dust behind, the object finally came to a rest in a patch of thorns some distance from the dropping zone. It was Yeti.

As the dust settled, an ambulance raced across the veld with its siren wailing. Right behind the ambulance was the Land Rover of Lieutenant Eddie. The vehicles stopped right beside Yeti who was standing in the veld in nothing but his underpants, slapping the dust and plants and grass and thorns from his body. His white woollen coat lay torn and shredded and strewn all over the dropping zone. The medics bundled Yeti into the ambulance and drove off, back to the Regiment. Not because Yeti was injured, but because people had come running to see what had happened and he was embarrassed to be standing around in only his skivvies.

"Are you completely crazy, Yeti?" asked Eddie as they all sat in his office drinking tea. "You can't jump out of an aircraft without a parachute."

"You told me that we were only jumping from six hundred feet above the ground," replied Yeti. "I didn't know that we were supposed to use parachutes."

"But didn't you see that all of us had parachutes on our backs before we jumped?" asked Jak.

"I thought they were your backpacks with tea and sandwiches and stuff," replied Yeti.

Everyone, except Yeti of course, packed up laughing so hard that they had tears in their eyes.

The telephone rang. Eddie answered the phone and was told that there was someone at the main gate to the Regiment that wanted to see him. Eddie went down to the gate and soon returned in the company of a policeman pushing a bicycle.

"This is Hennie," he said, introducing the policeman. "Constable Hennie van der Merwe of the S A P S. He wants to speak to you, Yeti."

"Well, I was just patrolling these *koeikampe* (cow pastures) around here," explained the policeman, "when I came across a huge big crack in the crust of the Earth. Now, this is destruction of government property and I have to arrest somebody. I believe you are responsible, Sir."

"Oh no!" groaned Jak. "This time we're going to jail, for sure."

"Listen, Constable," said Eddie. "We're actually thinking of building a dam on the *koeikamp*. If we have a dam it will provide water for our military base. With that crack in the ground we don't have to spend a lot of money excavating and building a dam. So, Yeti has really done us all a huge favour by providing the perfect solution to our problem."

After the policeman had left, Eddie's soldiers were seen returning to their barracks in the Regiment. When they heard the story of Yeti's jump, without a parachute, and the crack in the *koeikamp,* they too laughed so hard that the tears flowed freely.

If you go to Bloemfontein today you will see the dam in the *koiekamp* next to the military base. When it was eventually built, it was called *"Die Dam van Trane"*, or the Dam of Tears. Well, now you know why.

7

Meanwhile, back at the ranch …

In the olden days, when a chapter in a cowboy book began with the words "Meanwhile, back at the ranch…", the reader knew that he was about to learn of the activities of other characters in the story. Other than the hero, that is. So, in the same manner, this chapter will tell you about the progress and activities of the other contestants in the Great TREK.

Let us start with Bobby Breen, Humpty Dumpty, all the King's horses and all the King's men. Well, after a huge effort and terrible expense, this team with their Royal Colours, managed to reach the little town of Matjiesfontein on the fringe of the Great Karoo. There, waiting for them, was His Excellency, the very impatient and highly frustrated Ambassador of Great Britain and Northern Ireland to South Africa. The King of England had sent him in order to, as the King put it, "Get the show on the road." The Ambassador had thought long and hard about the problem. He thought he had the solution.

Standing at the Matjiesfontein railway station was a train loaded with hundreds and hundreds of hot air balloons. All the hot air balloons in South Africa, in fact. The Ambassador planned to load Bobby Breen, Humpty Dumpty and the whole entourage (remember that word?) onto the hot air balloons and to lift them into the sky where the wind would gently carry them all the way to the Limpopo River and ...**Victory**. For the King!

Well, it took another day and a half to feed and water all the horses, to prepare them for the journey and to load them into the baskets (called gondolas) hanging below the hot air balloons. It appeared as if the whole of the Karoo had come to see the spectacle.

There was further delay as a new crack in Humpty Dumpty's shell was repaired with vinegar and brown paper. At last, one by one, the balloons rose quietly and gracefully into the air. Soon there were hundreds and hundreds of balloons drifting across the open Karoo landscape, their bright colours dotting the cloudless sky like giant, magical airborne flowers. It was a magnificent and unforgettable sight. The Ambassador heaved a huge sigh of relief. That was when the trouble started.

All the pilots of the hot air balloons had told the Ambassador that they *could* reach the Limpopo River, not that they *would* reach the Limpopo River. What they had not told the Ambassador was that the winds over the Karoo are very fickle and unpredictable. Some days the wind blows from the East, on other days from the West, sometimes even from the South or the North. They also forgot to tell him that, on certain days, the wind could blow in different directions at different heights above the ground. That day was such a day.

The Ambassador watched as the great Armada of balloons rose higher and higher. The huge crowd of people on the ground clapped and cheered at the marvellous sight. The higher they went the stronger the wind blew. Then the balloons started drifting apart. Some went east. Some went west. Some went north. Some even drifted southwards, going back the way they had come. The Ambassador was stunned. His plan had failed, foiled by the ill winds – later to be known in South Africa as ***The Winds of Change***. He took off his magnificent top hat, threw it on the ground and stomped on it. His reputation and that of his government, like his hat, was ruined.

Bobby Breen and Humpty Dumpty were in a balloon that was drifting northwards, in the right direction. Bobby hoped and prayed that they would at least reach his hometown of Bloemfontein. There he would retire from the TREK and leave the huge task of collecting the scattered King's horses and King's men to his Excellency the Ambassador. It would take weeks and weeks.

Now, what about Kosie Koekemoer and Sterling Mustard? Well, they were lost. Hopelessly lost. Sterling was accustomed to navigating with his Doppler GPS in America, but it did not work in South Africa. In his efforts to avoid the traffic police, Sterling had been criss-crossing South Africa using all the little-known gravel roads, farm roads and bush tracks, some not even to be found on his map. They had stopped by the side of the road somewhere between the small towns of Hotazel and Lekkawarm, enjoying the sight of another glorious African sunset. Suddenly, a battered old bakkie (called a 'pick-up truck' in North America) pulled up in a cloud of dust. (At this stage you, the reader, must think that South Africa is the dustiest place on Earth).

A man in a short-sleeved khaki shirt, khaki shorts and velskoene without socks approached them. He smelled of sheep. Taking off his battered old brown army bush hat, he introduced himself. "Niklaas. Niklaas van der Merwe. Ek is 'n skaapboer van hierdie kontrei." (My name is Nicholas van der Merwe. I am a sheep farmer around here.)

Now, Niklaas was an Afrikaner. He spoke Afrikaans. He could barely understand a word of English and Sterling Mustard's American accent only added to the confusion.

"We're lost and looking for a place to sleep," said Sterling.

"Julle soek iemand om julle te sleep?" responded Niklaas. "Moenie worry nie, byt net vas!" (You're waiting for someone to give you a tow? Don't worry, just hang on.)

In less than 30 seconds, Sterling's smart racing car was hooked up to a tow-bar behind the bakkie. Soon afterwards they were racing across the *vlaktes* (the plains) in a cloud of dust (that dust again) as the sky slowly turned from pink, to red, to orange, to purple, to black.

At his farm-house Niklaas showed his guests to their quarters; Sterling's car was housed in a spacious, tidy garage with a couple of tractors. Kosie and Sterling were shown to a comfortable bedroom in the farmhouse.

"We can't stay too long," said Sterling. "We have to get on with the race."

"Ja, my vrou Martie is cooking for us 'n lekker skaapboud met aartappels en rys," replied Niklaas. (Yes, my wife Martha is cooking a nice leg of lamb with potatoes and rice).

"This should never have happened," sighed Sterling. "How I wish I had my Doppler."

"Dis reg," said Niklaas. "Kom ons gaan maak 'n dop. Ek het 'n lekker bottel Klippies daar op die stoep." (That's right. Let's have a dop (a drink). I have a nice bottle of brandy out on the verandah).

"Eishhh!" said Kosie, a typical African expression when registering dismay.

"Dis reg. Met ys," said Niklaas. "Met ys!" (That's right, with ice. With ice.)

It was going to be a long and confusing night.

Meanwhile, it was also getting dark in Stellenbosch. Dorothy Dunbar had gone for a long walk under the oak trees while Nastimania sat all by herself in the deserted courtyard of the hotel. She was waiting for midnight when her mangled spell would be broken and the rusty bucket, the pot-bellied pig, the purple rabbits and the smelly goats would all return to normal. The next morning she would be able to cast a really good spell and produce a really nice coach with fine horses, so that they could get on with the TREK.

A hotel porter by the name of Slimjan Febewarie (Cleverjohn February in English) saw a lady sitting in the courtyard. As he approached, Nastimania quickly turned herself into the elegant Queen Lilywhite. Slimjan knew that she was a "tourist", a royal one at that, and he was ever on the lookout for a quick buck.

"What about a nice cool glass of Val Japé, your honour?" he said, referring to that horrible sour white wine called *"vaaljapie"* that is made from the dregs of squashed grapes on the wine farms.

He would sell this cheap wine to her at the price of the finest Stellenbosch wine. He offered Nastimania a fine crystal champagne glass. She took one small sip that she spat out immediately before emptying the glass into a flowerbed.

"Don't you have anything better than this," she snapped. Slimjan scurried away to his locker where he kept a *"papsak"*, a five litre plastic bag of cheap sweet red wine that he sold to unsuspecting hotel guests as "Cape Sherry".

"Now this is nice," said Nastimania as she sipped the sweet wine. After the sour *vaaljapie* it was better, much better. But not good. After several glasses of the sweet wine Queen Lilywhite was feeling generous.

"Where is your vehicle?" she asked Slimjan.

The porter went off to fetch the rickety old bicycle that he used to cycle to work each day. On the way back he stopped off at his locker, filled the Queen's glass before taking a huge mouthful of wine from the *papsak.* While the porter was away Nastimania found a fat old cat sitting in the shadows, a box of empty wine bottles and a bag full of kitchen scraps. When Slimjan returned to the courtyard she lined him up next to his bike and the rest of the stuff she had found. Then, with a flourish she produced her magic wand from the wide sleeve of her robe. She quickly took a peek at the magic word on the scrap of paper in her shoe then waved her wand at the startled hotel porter. **"RAMBAKAZAM!"** she cried.

POOF! The porter's bike turned into a magnificent red Ford Mustang convertible. Slimjan was suddenly dressed in a smart black dinner jacket with a starched white shirt and a black bow-tie. The scruffy old cat had become a smartly dressed waiter and the fleas on the cat had all turned into musicians in an orchestra playing softly in a corner on fine musical instruments. The wine box had become a table with two chairs. The kitchen scraps were converted into wonderful dishes of fish, meat, vegetables, fresh fruit and dessert.

The waiter served dinner to Queen Lilywhite and Slimjan as they listened to the pleasant music, drank the horrid *soet wyn* (sweet wine) from Slimjan's papsak and spoke about important world events, like the next rugby test match between the Springboks and the All Blacks.

At midnight the spell was broken.

The next morning Slimjan woke up with a dreadful headache. He was lying on the hard cobblestones in the courtyard next to his rickety old bicycle with his arms around a scruffy old cat with fleas crawling happily all over his body. Despite his throbbing head he smiled at the memories of a wonderful dream.

BANG. BANG. BANG. It was Dorothy Dunbar banging at Nastimania's door. **BANG. BANG. BANG**, louder than before.

"Come on, Queen Lilywhite! Wake up! We have to get moving," called Dorothy.

Nastimania woke up with a terrible headache. Her eyes were swollen, her nose was blocked and her tongue was thick and furry from the horrible sweet red wine. Her head was spinning, her tummy was rumbling and she was on the point of throwing up. She had a serious case of *wingerdgriep,* "vineyard influenza", remember?

Desperately she looked under her bed. There, to her great relief, was the shoebox. She opened it. With bleary eyes she peered at Fungus the frog, the five white mice, the three trolls disguised as grasshoppers and the tribe of fleas. Oh, how she wished that she had not drunk that horrid sweet red wine last night. She so badly did not want to disappoint Dorothy Dunbar again.

Quickly Nastimania dressed as Queen Lilywhite.

"Wait for me in the dining room, Dorothy," she called through the locked door.

When Dorothy left, Nastimania took the shoebox and hurried down to the courtyard where she saw Slimjan stumbling off home, pushing his bike. She quickly packed out the shoebox, placing the frog, the mice, the grasshoppers and the fleas in a row. She took the scrap of paper from her shoe. She tried to read the magic word, but the letters were blurred, swimming in front of her eyes. She concentrated and stared at the magic word. She concentrated even harder. She could hear the footsteps of Dorothy Dunbar as she approached the courtyard, tired of waiting in the dining room. She read the magic password one last time. She took the magic wand, wiped it on her sleeve for good luck, lifted it above her head and said the magic password, "RAMBAKAZANG!"

Was that the right password? Close! Very Close! But not close enough.

KERBONK! The shoebox turned into a stunning royal coach drawn by four magnificent white horses. Beside the coach Prince Bandilegs was mounted on his beautiful white stallion. The grasshoppers had turned into pageboys in really fancy clothes and the tribe of fleas had become a military band just ready to play a royal fanfare.

Queen Lilywhite was overjoyed. Dorothy Dunbar was speechless. But so was everyone else. In fact the whole scene, except Dorothy and Queen

Lilywhite of course, had turned into statues of white marble.

Nothing moved. Not a sound. Not a twitch. Queen Lilywhite sank to her knees as her headache hammered away. Dorothy turned, sighed heavily and headed towards town for another long walk under the oak trees of Stellenbosch.

A chirpy little *mossie* (a sparrow) landed on Prince Bandilegs' stony head … and pooped on his hat.

8

Yeti in the Mountain Kingdom

While the rest of the contestants in the Great TREK were floating around all over South Africa in hot air balloons, getting lost in the dry North-West district of Hotazel or drinking sweet red wine in Stellenbosch, Jak and his friends were the heroes of all the paratroopers in Bloemfontein. Never before had there been anyone that jumped from an aircraft without a parachute … and survived. Yeti was voted as the paratrooper's "Man Amongst Men" and a huge party was held in his honour. At the party he was presented with a brand-new white coat of South African Angora wool … especially knitted for him by the Regimental Ladies Club, many of them the ladies that packed the parachutes for use by the Regiment.

Even though Yeti had not used one of their packed parachutes, they still felt responsible for his safety.

The day after the party, Lieutenant Eddie came over to see Jak, Yeti and Dodgy while they were having breakfast.

"I have just been to see the OC," he said, with a grim look on his face.

"What did she want?" asked Jak.

Eddie gave Jak a smack on the back of his head. "Not the *ousie,* stupid! The O.C. The Officer Commanding. The Boss." (*Ousie* is an African word meaning "eldest sister". It is often politely used by children when addressing adult African ladies).

"Oh. What did **he** want?" replied Jak with a big smile on his dial.

"Well, there's a problem with a not-very-big tribe of people over in Lesotho. Lesotho is land-locked, which means that it is completely surrounded by South Africa. So, everything they need comes through South Africa. Their land is mostly in the Maluti and the Drakensberg Mountains, so everyone calls it the Mountain Kingdom," Eddie explained.

"Ah!" said Yeti. "I know all about mountain kingdoms. What is the problem? How can we help you?"

"Well," responded Eddie, "the leader of this tribe is a young man by the name of Lepoqo (pronounced lee-pó-coo). He led his people into the mountains to escape the fighting and the cattle theft that have been going on around here. Now there is a Chief of another tribe, his name is Moeletsi (pronounced moo-let-see), and he wants to take over Lepoqo's kingdom."

"Yup, I know all about that. Queen Lilywhite is forever trying to take over my Kingdom," said Yeti. "Come on, Eddie, let's get over there and give this young man a hand."

"Well," said Eddie, "the OC is sending me over there with my platoon to see what gives. If we can solve the problem, we will. If not, we'll have to get more troops to come and help us. The OC says that you can all come along … as long as you stay out of trouble."

Dodgy's ears were drooping and he didn't look very happy at all.

"I may not be a soldier," he said in a miserable voice, "but I am a goat and I know manure when I smell it. This doesn't smell good."

Well, soon Lieutenant Eddie and his paratroopers were bustling about getting all their equipment and food and cars and trucks and tents and radios and so on prepared for their mission. In no time at all they were ready to roll. After a nice cup of tea and sandwiches, Eddie and Jak and Yeti and Dodgy were seen driving away in Eddie's jeep. They were leading a convoy of five trucks loaded with paratroopers and their equipment in the direction of Lesotho, the Mountain Kingdom.

Meanwhile, up in the mountains, Lepoqo led his people up a mountain with a flat top. The mountain had very steep sides with only one path leading to the top. The people took plenty of cattle, goats and other food so that they could survive on the mountain for a long time. There was also a fountain on the mountain, so there was enough water for all the animals and all the people to drink. The name of the mountain was Thaba Bosiu.

When Eddie and the soldiers arrived at the mountain, it was completely surrounded by the warriors of Chief Moeletsi. They were all carrying shields and assegais and *knopkieries* (fighting sticks with a big knob at one end) and looked really dangerous. There were huts all around the bottom of the mountain, there were hundreds of cattle and goats and there were huge piles of food stacked all around. There were special stacks of wooden barrels with drinking water all over. Yeti took Eddie to one side and told him that they should wait until dark and then clamber up onto the mountain without being seen. When the sun went down, that is what they did.

Lepoqo was very pleased to see Eddie and the paratroopers. He was surprised and overjoyed when he was introduced to Jak, Yeti and Dodgy. He told them that he was expecting Chief Moeletsi to attack his mountain during the night or early the next day.

"I have many women and children here on this mountain," he told them. "I don't want to fight Chief Moeletsi, but I have to protect my people from harm."

"Don't worry, Lepoqo," said Yeti. "I've had the same problem back home from time to time. I know how to deal with the situation. All of you can go to bed. Eddie and his paratroopers will stand guard during the night while Jak, Dodgy and I make certain preparations."

Down at the foot of the mountain Moeletsi and his warriors were preparing to attack the top of the mountain at sunrise the next morning. On the top of the mountain Lepoqo and his people were getting a good night's sleep. The paratroopers were on guard as Jak, Yeti and Dodgy collected a huge pile of big round stones and massive round boulders that they placed at the top of the path leading up the mountain.

Well, I guess you know what happened. As the sun rose the next morning the warriors at the foot of the mountain let out a bloodcurdling war-cry and started rushing up the path leading to the top of the mountain. The bravest warriors led the way. Jak and Dodgy were peering over the crest of the mountain while Yeti stationed himself beside the pile of rocks and boulders.

Jak waited until the warriors were half-way up the path.

"OK, Yeti! Let 'em have it!" he cried.

Yeti picked up the biggest, heaviest boulder that he could find and lifted it above his head. He stood there for a while until he was sure that all the attacking warriors had seen him. With a great roar the huge white-clad monster threw the boulder down onto the pathway. Then, with a big smile on his face, Yeti started pushing the enormous round boulders and rocks over the edge of the mountain onto the pathway too. There was an almighty rumbling sound as the rocks and boulders rushed and tumbled down the mountainside, sweeping everything away before them. When the warriors saw the huge boulders racing down upon them there was total confusion. Some threw away their assegais and *knobkerries* as they jumped out of the way. Others turned and raced down the mountain to escape. Yeti kept pushing and shoving the boulders and rocks over the edge until there were none left. He then joined Jak, Dodgy and Eddie where they stood laughing at the antics of the warriors as they made desperate efforts to get out of the way of the big stones.

And that was not the end. As the huge round boulders came rushing down from the top of the mountain, they knocked down Moeletsi's huts and kraals like matchsticks, they smashed the water barrels, they scattered the herds of cattle and goats and all the horses and they sent the herders and cooks and bottle washers running away into the veld to save their lives. When the warriors got to the bottom of the mountain, they did not stop to tell Moeletsi what had happened. Oh no! They just kept running. They would never, ever forget the terrible sight of Yeti standing on the mountain with the huge boulder held above his head.

Now, the young Lepoqo was a clever young man and also a good diplomat. He asked Eddie to go down to Chief Moeletsi, in his devastated camp, and ask him if he would be so kind as to meet with Lepoqo that afternoon. Moeletsi was a nasty man, but he was not stupid. He had no horse, he had no food, he had no water and all his warriors had run away. He agreed to meet with Lepoqo that afternoon.

As the sun started getting low on the horizon, Moeletsi sat on an anthill combing his beard. In *his* tribe only the most important men were allowed to have a beard and Moeletsi considered himself to be *The Most Important Man*. He was very proud of his thick, curly black beard, also of his magnificent clothes of lion and leopard skins and ostrich feathers. Around his neck he wore a necklace of leopard claws and warthog tusks. On his head he wore the ring of dark polished wood, almost like a crown, indicating that he was a Chief.

Soon he saw a small party approaching his lonely anthill. It consisted of Lepoqo, Eddie, Jak, Yeti, Dodgy and a group of young boys and girls carrying clay pots on their head. Moeletsi could not hide his surprise when he was introduced to Yeti. He was even more surprised, almost wetting his pants, when Yeti shook his hand, almost crushing his fingers in a grip of steel. After shaking hands, very gently, with everyone else, he was overjoyed when the boys and girls gently laid down the pots around the anthill. They were filled with the cool and delicious local beer made from fermented goat's milk mixed with ground sorghum.

After a long and pleasant gulp of beer, Moeletsi's fingers started feeling a lot better. Several more gulps and he was congratulating Lepoqo on his brilliant military tactics in defending his mountain fort. When Lepoqo told Moeletsi that he would be allowed to leave Lesotho to return to his own land unharmed, he drank a whole pot of beer to celebrate. Soon no one could understand what Moeletsi was saying as his face was buried in another pot of beer.

Very politely, everyone withdrew back to the top of the mountain to celebrate their victory with a big feast. Only Lepoqo remained behind to see that Chief Moeletsi was comfortable for the night, as he had fallen asleep next to the anthill. With him was one young boy with the last pot of beer that was placed by Moeletsi's side so that he would have something to drink when he woke up the next morning. There were no vineyards in Lesotho, which meant that Moeletsi would awake with a serious *babbalas,* the local equivalent of *vineyard influenza.*

As you may well imagine, there was a big party on the top of that mountain. The bonfires could be seen for miles around. There was plenty of singing and dancing and telling of stories. Everyone thought that the best story was the one of Yeti rolling the huge boulders down the side of the mountain to frighten off Moeletsi's warriors. Everyone? No, not everyone!

"That's not the best story!" a small voice was heard to say. It was the young boy that carried the last pot of beer that was left for Chief Moeletsi.

"Let me tell you the best story of all!"

The boy then went on to tell everyone how Lepoqo had taken his razor and had shaved off the beard of Chief Moeletsi while he lay sleeping ... after drinking all that beer.

"It was a wonderful sight to see," said the young boy. "And I will never forget that sound."

"What sound?" the people asked.

"Shwe, Shwe," he hissed, imitating the actions and the sound of the razor scraping off Moeletsi's beard. Everyone screamed with laughter.

Well, poor old Moeletsi returned to his land unharmed, but he had to hide away for many months to allow his beard to grow again. Unfortunately everyone had heard the story and laughed at him behind his back. He was no longer the bully that he had been before. The warriors that had run away from Thaba Bosiu were too ashamed to return home, so Moeletsi's army became very weak. He never again tried to take over the Kingdom of Lesotho.

From that day onwards, in honour of his heroic act, Lepoqo was known as Moshweshwe – reminding everyone of the sound of his razor shaving off the beard of the ruthless bully. As the years went by, he became famous as the wise old leader of the Kingdom of Lesotho and his name slowly changed to Moshesh, as it is to this very day.

9

The Big Hole

The people of Lesotho were still celebrating the great victory over Chief Moeletsi as Jak, Yeti and Dodgy made their way back to Bloemfontein. The paratroopers had left some three days earlier, but Yeti and Dodgy wanted to have a look at the Golden Gate on the border between Lesotho and the Free State. They were very disappointed when they found that the "Gold" was actually red, orange and yellow sandstone and that the "Gate" was the valley between the high cliffs of sandstone eroded by a river over the centuries. South Africa's Grand Canyon ... well, sort of.

"I thought we were going to see real gold," grumbled the unhappy Dodgy. "Everyone says that

South Africa is such a fabulously rich country, but all I've seen is dust."

"There is plenty of gold here in the Free State," said Jak, "but we have to go down a mine shaft a mile or even deeper underground to find it. Do you want to do that?"

"Underground?" asked Yeti. "You want me to go underground? Not on your life! Where I come from we have a saying that goes like this; "what goes up must come down". I believe that, because that is how gravity works! But I also know that what goes down often stays down, so you won't get me to go down a mine shaft very easily."

"OK, so what about diamonds?" asked Jak. "Here in the Free State we have plenty of diamonds. You just dig a hole in the ground, take out the gravel, sift it and very often you will find diamonds."

"That sounds like a much better idea," said Dodgy. "Let's go looking for diamonds!"

So off they went, all the way to Kimberley, which is not really in the Free State, but which is the centre of diamond mining in the world. Unfortunately a lot of other people also had the bright idea of mining for diamonds around Kimberley. There were hundreds, no, thousands of miners from all over the world, all looking for diamonds. Every miner had a little plot of ground, called a "claim", where he was allowed to dig. Jak, Yeti and Dodgy went along to the mining office and asked to be given a claim, where they could start digging.

"Do you already know which claim you want?" asked the official.

"Oh no," replied Jak, "we've only just arrived. I'm from the Bushveld and I just wanted to show my visitors from the Kingdom of Shangri-La how easy it is to get rich in South Africa."

The official looked at the three friends, the most unlikely of diamond diggers, and laughed. "All right," he said, "you can have a piece of land outside town where there are a lot of foreign visitors who also want to get rich quick."

He smiled because they looked so harmless. He didn't think that they'd last very long.

When Yeti and his pals arrived at their claim it was getting dark. Somehow they had expected to find a pleasant spot with water close by, with trees and grass and maybe a little hut to stay in. What they found was a piece of flat, stony, dusty dirt with a few scraggly bushes that would not even feed a hungry goat. Making the best of a bad situation, they pitched their tent, had a cold supper, a sip of water and then lay down on the hard ground to get some sleep. Tomorrow, they told one another, they would make their fortune.

The next day dawned bright and sunny. After a cold breakfast the three friends decided to start mining.

All around them they could hear the sounds of other miners digging away at the hard, dry ground, shifting gravel, moving dirt and sifting sand.

"So, what do we do now?" asked Dodgy, not in the least interested in slaving away under the hot sun.

"We dig," said Yeti, rolling up his sleeves.

"With what?" asked Jak.

The man who was making the most money on the Diamond Fields was the one selling picks and shovels and other tools. He made even more money as Jak bought three picks, three shovels, three buckets and a sieve to sift the gravel.

That evening, as it grew dark, Dodgy fell asleep without even eating a cold supper. Jak and Yeti discussed the day's work.

"Look at my poor hands. I have blisters on top of blisters. There has to be a better way of digging out the gravel," said Jak.

"There is," replied Yeti. "Dynamite!"

'Oh my soul," said Jak. "Dynamite explodes, doesn't it? Do you know anything about dynamite?"

Yeti shook his head. "Nope, I know nothing about dynamite. But what can be so difficult? You dig a little hole, you put dynamite in it and you blow it up. Then you take the gravel out of the hole and you sift it. What's so difficult about that?"

With thoughts of a much easier way of finding diamonds, Jak and Yeti drifted off into deep and well-earned sleep.

The following day Jak, Yeti and Dodgy visited all their neighbours asking each one for a bit of dynamite. A Scottish prospector gave them one stick; a broken one. An American miner gave them two sticks. A Chinaman, who made fireworks in China before coming to Kimberley to seek his fortune, gave them a brown packet full of homemade gunpowder, which is much the same as dynamite – it explodes. An Englishman, who was sadly giving up his claim to go home, gave them a box full of dynamite sticks. An Irishman gave them one stick of dynamite, but he also had about twenty sticks that had gotten wet when he fell into the river on his way to Kimberley.

"I tried one of the wet sticks when I arrived," said the Irishman. "It went off like a damp squid. You can have these twenty sticks that remained. Maybe they'll work for you."

Well, our three diamond-digging friends trudged around the whole day collecting dynamite. When Dodgy, who was pulling a small cart loaded with the dynamite, started complaining, they went back home.

"Be careful with all that dynamite," called a friendly Canadian as they passed his claim in the late afternoon. "Don't use too much!" But nobody bothered to tell them how much was too much.

On their claim they carefully stacked all the dynamite outside their tent. They then had a nice supper of soup and bread before falling asleep to dream of all the diamonds they would find the next day.

Next morning Jak was the first to wake. Quietly he left the tent and started digging a hole to pack the dynamite in. When the hole was ready he took a stick of dynamite and placed it at the bottom. It looked so small. Just then Yeti and Dodgy joined him. They all looked at the thin little stick of dynamite at the bottom of the hole.

"That's not enough," said Dodgy. "We don't want to make hundreds of explosions all day. Let's make one big explosion once a day, and then spend the rest of the day picking up the diamonds."

"He's right," said Yeti.

"So, how much dynamite should we use?" asked Jak.

They decided that five sticks would be enough. Then they added three more sticks to the pile in the bottom of the hole, one for each of them ... just in case. And one for luck. Nine sticks of dynamite at the bottom of the hole still didn't look to be enough, but they decided to be cautious.

"OK," said Jak, "we'd better warn our neighbours that we're going to make an explosion.

Yeti, you prepare the fuse while Dodgy and I go around warning everyone else that we're going to blow up the dynamite at ten o'clock." Off they went.

Yeti started preparing the fuse before covering up the dynamite sticks.

"I'd better add two more sticks, just in case," he said to himself. "And one for luck," he said, tossing another stick of dynamite into the hole. He then covered up the hole with sand and gravel with the fuse sticking out of the ground, ready to be lit.

Jak returned from warning the neighbours. He saw the fuse sticking out of the ground. Yeti was around the back of the tent washing his hands. That dynamite is not going to be enough, Jak thought to himself. So he made a little hole in the sand, right next to the fuse, and added two more sticks – and one more for luck. He then went off to join Yeti in washing his hands.

Dodgy returned from warning the neighbours. He saw the fuse sticking out of the ground. His friends were around the back of the tent washing their hands. That dynamite is not going to be enough, Dodgy thought to himself. So he made a little hole in the sand, right next to the fuse, and added three more sticks – and one more for luck.

At half past nine, with thirty minutes to go before ten o'clock, Yeti lit the fuse and then followed Jak and Dodgy to a little rise some distance from their claim. There they would stand and watch the explosion before returning to pick up the diamonds. Then they saw that all the miners and other prospectors were walking or riding bicycles and horses in the direction of Kimberley.

"Where is everyone going," Jak asked the Scotsman who had given them their first (broken) stick of dynamite.

'Haven't you heard?" replied the Scotsman. "It's Saturday today and the Springboks are playing a rugby match against the Wallabies at the De Beers Stadium in Kimberley this afternoon. Come along! This doesn't happen very often around here. Everyone will be at the match, so no one is going to steal your diamonds. You can return later this afternoon and start mining again."

Jak was a huge supporter of the Springboks, so the three friends decided to join the crowd on their way to town. It would also be a great experience for Yeti and Dodgy who had never seen rugby match before – and a match between South Africa and Australia is always a lot of fun, often with a few fights thrown in just to make it interesting. Everyone was in a very happy mood and there was a lot of joking and laughing and singing as the crowd made their way to the centre of Kimberley.

On the stroke of ten o'clock, long before the match started, there was a puff of smoke on the horizon followed by a huge explosion as nineteen sticks of dynamite (did you count them?) blew up.

Then there was another explosion, this time about one hundred times larger than the first, as the stack of dynamite standing beside the tent was detonated.

The earth shook as if an earthquake was taking place. A massive cloud of smoke and dust and rocks and boulders and sand and gravel and stones rose up into the air like a giant mushroom. The shock wave from the explosion threw everyone to the ground. All the windowpanes in all the houses in Kimberley were shattered. Tiles lifted off the roofs. Dogs barked and all the other animals ran around in panic. Ladies screamed and babies cried. The sky grew dark as the cloud covered the sun.

Remember Yeti saying that everything that goes up must come down? Well, that is what happened next. It started raining sand and gravel and stones and rocks and boulders as all the debris came back to earth in a huge, brown waterfall. Everyone got up and then just stood and stared. Not a word was said, but all the miners were looking at Jak, Yeti and Dodgy. Then everyone went closer and had a look at the biggest man-made hole in the world; 1 500 feet in diameter and 3000 feet deep. That is three times deeper than the Eiffel Tower in Paris is tall.

Now, many people will tell you that miners prospecting for diamonds dug the Big Hole at Kimberley by hand, using shovels. Well, they may be right, because the miners certainly moved all the gravel and dirt that had been blown up into the air by the giant explosion. Many miners became rich, almost instantaneously, from the diamonds that they found while sifting through the rubble.

They would have thanked Jak and Yeti and Dodgy for their good fortune, but our three friends were nowhere to be found. They had wisely decided to continue with the Great TREK and were far, far away – with not even a single diamond to show for their efforts.

10

Battling through to Bloemfontein

(This is one of those "meanwhile, back at the ranch" chapters.)

While Jak, Yeti and Dodgy were changing the South African landscape forever, what was happening to the other Great TREK contenders? In a word – NOTHING. But that is not to say that they weren't having some adventures of their own. Oh no! Far from it.

Kosie Koekemoer and Sterling Mustard were hopelessly lost in the dry sheep-farming districts of South Africa. Their biggest problem was the traditionally friendly and hospitable South African farmers. Whenever they stopped to ask for directions the farmer would insist that they stay over for the night. The next problem was one of language. Most of the farmers could not speak a word of English. Kosie was fluent in Afrikaans, but Sterling Mustard could neither speak nor understand a word of the language.

So, after spending the night on a farm and after a huge, traditional South African sheep-farmers breakfast, a farmer would tell them, "*Volg die pad tot by die T-aansluiting en draai links. Oraait?*" (Follow the road to the T-junction and turn left, all right?)

Kosie and Sterling would follow the directions to the T-junction.

"Turn left here!" says Kosie.

"No ways," replies Sterling, "I distinctly heard the man say that we should turn RIGHT. Who's driving anyway?"

So they turn right … and get lost yet again. They stop at a farm to ask for directions, meet the traditionally friendly and hospitable South African farmer, and end up spending the night. And so on.

Bobby Breen and Humpty-Dumpty somehow managed to make it to Bloemfontein in their hot air balloon. They were slightly disappointed not to create a sensation when they landed on the main rugby field at Grey College on a Saturday afternoon. There were literally thousands of people there to watch the annual rugby match between Grey and Affies (an Afrikaans boys high school) from Pretoria. Unfortunately, the spectators were far more interested in the rugby than in some fat oke in fancy dress arriving in a balloon and very quickly removed the balloon, its basket and its passengers from the field so that the rugby could continue. While Grey College and their supporters noisily celebrated the 44 – 3 win over Affies, Bobby and Humpty-Dumpty calmly walked off to Bobby's house, where they found his parents watching the celebrations of the Grey-Affies match on TV.

While they were watching TV, Bobby converted his parents' living room into a military-style "operations room" with maps and computers and additional telephones and fax machines. Soon they were telephoning all over the country trying to locate the scattered King's horses and King's men. Every time they located some, they marked the spot on the map with a red pin.

After several days of searching, their map was covered in red pins. Cape Town, Springbok, Pofadder, Upington, Port Elizabeth, Underberg, Virginia. On and on it went; King's horses and King's men all over the country.

"Oh no," groaned Bobby with his head in his hands. "How are we ever going to put them all together again?"

Dorothy Dunbar from Durban had somehow managed to keep Queen Lilywhite away from the *dop* (booze). Furthermore, by some miracle, she and her strange group from the Kingdom of Herenthere had managed to stagger into Bloemfontein. It was while Dorothy was searching for a place for them all to stay, that she bumped into Bobby Breen in Maitland Street, Bloemfontein's main street.

"We have a nice Granny-flat at home," said Bobby. "You're welcome to come and stay with us for a while."

"Does your dad brew beer or make wine or *witblits* (moonshine) or stuff like that?" asked Dorothy.

"No!" said Bobby.

"Thank you. We'd love to spend a day or two with you," said Dorothy with a sigh of relief.

The people of Bloemfontein did not even bat an eyelid as the strange procession made its way down Maitland Street. When they saw the white horses drawing the magnificent coach with Queen Lilywhite inside waving graciously at the spectators and Prince Bandilegs on a prancing white stallion, they thought that it was all just a rehearsal for the University Rag Parade.

Right behind the little procession came the sound of a powerful car making a lot of noise, revving up its huge 7-litre V8 engine. Only then did the people of Bloemfontein show any interest as a bright red and yellow racing car rumbled noisily down Maitland Street. It was Sterling Mustard and Kosie Koekemoer that had somehow managed to extricate themselves from the dusty maze of South African farm roads to arrive in Bloemfontein. Bobby Breen also invited them to stay at his parent's home for a few days, an invitation which they readily accepted.

That evening, as Bobby and Kosie and Dorothy sat on the lawn waiting for the *tjops* (lamb chops) and *wors* (sausage) to *braai* (cook on the barbeque), Bobby said, "I've invited you all to stay here so that we can solve our problems together. If we don't do something soon, Jak and Yeti and Dodgy are going to win this race."

They called Sterling and Humpty-Dumpty and Queen Lilywhite and Prince Bandilegs to join in their discussions. Fortunately they came up with a plan of action before the stroke of midnight and Queen Lilywhite and Bandilegs were able to hide in her room before they turned into Nastimania and Fungus the frog.

The plan was for Kosie and Sterling to drive to the spots on the map where there were red pins. There they would gather together the King's horses and King's men and wait for the train to pick them up. Train? What train?

Well, Queen Lilywhite announced that she would arrange for the train. Actually, as Nastimania with her magic wand, she would turn the shoebox into a train. Fungus the frog would become the driver.

Greaseball, Meatball and Furball would become the conductor, the baggage master and the bedding boy. When all the King's horses and all the King's men had been found and loaded onto the train, they would proceed to Bloemfontein to pick up Bobby Breen and Humpty-Dumpty. Once everyone was on the train, they would all travel up to Pretoria together where they would re-start the Great TREK.

Queen Lilywhite was very enthusiastic and said that she would arrange for the train to be painted in the colours of her team. Do you still remember what those colours were? Yup, that's right! White and pink and baby blue with a splash of silver and a touch of gold. She also decided that she would call the train … the Blue Train.

That was the plan.

11

The Blue Train

Bloemfontein is a very exciting city, but only if you go to school at Grey College or if you really love rugby. It is the capital city of what used to be known as the Orange Free State, so-called because the reddish-brown dust turns everything orange, nothing is free and the roads are in a terrible state. Queen Lilywhite knew nothing about rugby and Grey College being the best **boys** school in South Africa, perhaps even in the entire world, so Bloemfontein was not really the place for her. There was nothing much for her to do as she had tried the local beer, called mabele, and (unlike "Without-a-beard" Moeletsi in Lesotho) found it rather gruesome. So, she spent a long time thinking about the trip she was about to make all around the country in the Blue Train. To make such a special trip you need a very special train, so she spent a lot of time designing the Blue Train in her mind, preparing for her magic spell. Did you know that she really liked trains?

On Monday morning Queen Lilywhite woke up (well, actually it was Nastimania that woke up, but you know what I mean). She was very excited. She was about to create a masterpiece. And what's more, she was going to travel all around South Africa in that masterpiece – a luxury train. She was up early. She flew across to the train-station on her broom and was soon busy unpacking all the contents of her shoebox. Out came Fungus the frog, the three Balls (Greaseball, Meatball and Furball) in the shape of grasshoppers, the white mice and a handful of fleas. When all was ready she changed into the Queen, stood on her tippy-toes, took a last peek at her magic password and then closed her eyes tightly while imagining exactly what she was about to create. Slowly she lifted her magic wand above her head. Then, with an artistic flick of her wrist, she cried **RAMBAKAZAM**!

POOF! There on the station in Bloemfontein stood the most magnificent train the world had ever seen. It was a nice sky blue in colour with a white roof, large windows, dark blue curtains with trimmings of pink and silver and gold around the doors and windows and all along the edges of the coaches. The engine was huge. It was gleaming silver with all the extra bits in gold. Standing on the footplate (that is where the driver stands when the train is in the station) was Prince Bandilegs (actually it was Fungus parading as Bandilegs parading as the driver). On the nose of the engine was its name, *THE BLUE TRAIN*, in royal-blue-and-silver letters. It was a spectacular sight.

The crowds clapped and cheered and waved as the Blue Train pulled out of the station. All the coaches were empty, of course, as the train still had to collect its passengers from all over the country. So, there was only one passenger on the train. That was Queen Lilywhite in the VIP coach that Nastimania had designed for a Queen, in fact for herself.

The coach had a large comfortable bed, a golden bath with a golden basin and a golden toilet, a beautiful sitting room with the finest furniture, beautiful paintings, Persian carpets and silk curtains. There was also a fine bar but, as Nastimania could not make beer or wine or whiskey or any of that stuff with her crumby wand, it was of no real use. Note to myself, thought Nastimania – buy a much fancier magic wand on E-Bay when we get back home.

First the train went down to Natal where Kosie Koekemoer and Sterling McQueen had found many of the King's horses and the King's men. Most of them were on the golden beaches of Durban enjoying the delightful South African sun. When they heard that they were going back to Pretoria in a train they were not happy. Many of them had been on troop-trains before and did not look forward to repeating the experience. There was no way of knowing if **ALL** the King's horses and **ALL** the King's men actually boarded the train in Durban, and I am convinced that many of them "missed" the train and just stayed on the beaches. In fact I believe that many of their descendants can still be found on Durban's beaches to this very day (although some of them may have drifted across the ocean to Bondi Beach in Australia or to Long Beach, California).

Once the King's horses and the King's men were on the train, the problems started. It had nothing to do with the train or the food. The problem was with Nastimania's spell. Remember, her magic spell only lasted until midnight, when everything turned back to normal again. So, imagine being on a train full of soldiers and horses, travelling at the speed of the wind across the veld, and on the stroke of midnight the train turns into a shoebox. Imagine that spectacular prang! … called a train-wreck North America

Queen Lilywhite had her hands full with angry soldiers and stubborn horses that were woken up every night just before midnight, marched some distance into the veld to pitch their tents where they would sleep until daybreak the next day. Then they would break camp, march back to the railway line and board the train once more. Fortunately all the King's men were very well trained and disciplined and soon fell into the strange routine.

Queen Lilywhite was the one with nervous stress, with not a beer or a glass of wine in sight. On and on it went, day after day, night after night; picking up the scattered King's horses and King's men. At last there was only one group left; all those that had landed in and around Cape Town. Kosie and Sterling, remembering what had happened in Durban, managed to round them all up and had them staying in a little town in the mountains East of Cape Town.

The Blue Train puffed merrily along, on its way back across the Karoo to the little town of Franchhoek. This is the place in the Cape Province where all the French people settled when they fled from France to South Africa many years ago. The French, as you know (well, maybe you don't, but now you do) are world famous for their wonderful wine. When they came to South Africa they brought plenty of vine cuttings with them, which they then planted in their new homeland. Today the Cape Province is covered in vineyards that were started by the early French settlers called the Huguenots.

When the Blue Train puffed into Franchhoek station, the people cheered wildly. They weren't really happy to see the train, they were happy to know that the train would soon be removing the King's horses and the King's men. Why, you ask? Well, have you ever **smelt the pong** that horses and soldiers make after a few days?

The people of Franchhoek were so pleased, that they decided to have a big celebration. Because South Africans are so polite and so hospitable, they also invited Queen Lilywhite, Kosie, Sterling and all the King's horses and all the King's men to the party. Well, I guess you know what happened. Yup, that's right! ***MARAKKAS*** (an Afrikaans word, which means confusion, chaos and disaster).

It all started at the party, with the toasts. This is what people do at a party or wedding or other celebrations. They fill their glasses with champagne, which is bubbly French wine, then someone stands up, raises his glass and says. "Good Health to Zayden!" or "God Bless Canada!" or *"Viva, Afrika, Viva*!" or something like that. Everyone then stands up, repeats the toast in a loud voice before drinking the champagne. After a while someone else stands up, proposes a toast and the whole thing is repeated.

Well, the Mayor of Franchhoek was a very jolly fellow and enjoyed a good party. When he was not busy being the Mayor he was a plumber, so he had lots of money (even more than a doctor) and gave plenty of parties. He stood up and, in his pompous Mayor's voice, he proposed a toast to Queen Lilywhite and the other foreign visitors. Queen Lilywhite loved toasts.

Well, that's not strictly correct; Queen Lilywhite loved champagne. She jumped to her feet (but not before having her glass refilled with champagne) and proposed a toast to the Mayor and the wonderful people of Franchhoek. The Mayor bounced back and proposed a toast to the wonderful people of the Kingdom of Herenthere. Queen Lilywhite raised her glass to all the good people of South Africa. The Mayor raised his glass to all the King's Horses and all the King's men. Queen Lilywhite raised hers to the magnificent Blue Train. On and on it went, toast after toast after toast. Eventually all the guests had left and the King's men went back to their tents to prepare for an early morning departure on the grand Blue Train. Only the Queen and the Mayor remained at the party, still toasting the flowers and the birds and the bees and the butterflies and the cockroaches and anything else they could think of.

Later that night, well after midnight, a porter sweeping the platform at the railway-station found a bedraggled old woman (Nastimania) fast asleep on a wooden bench on the platform, covered in a dusty cloak and with a pointy, battered old black hat on her head. There was an old broom and a shoebox under the bench. He tried to shoo the old woman away, but she was sleeping so soundly and snoring so loudly that he let her be.

The next morning, long before the sun was up, Nastimania awoke to the sound of men and horses arriving at the station, preparing for a train journey to Pretoria. There was clanging and banging, shouting and cursing, laughing and neighing, kicking and bucking.

To Nastimania it sounded like a circus parade marching through her head. She groaned, sat upright on the bench, tried to stand up on her feet but promptly fell down in a dusty heap on the platform. She knew that she had to have the Blue Train ready to receive all the King's horses and all the King's men. She also knew that she was in trouble.

Stumbling about, Nastimania removed everything from the old shoebox and lined it all up next to the railway line; the frog, the grasshoppers, the mice and the fleas. She then took up the magic wand and wiped it once under her armpit. She removed the note from her shoe, only to find that some champagne that she had spilt the night before had smudged the ink. She tried to read the word, but it was faint and blurry. She squinted her eyes, but that did not help. She wracked her brain (what was left of it), but the magic password would not come to her. Eventually she stood on the steps to the station, stopped a passing labourer on his way to work and asked him to read the scrap of paper from her shoe. The best he could do was "ramblakamba". Nastimania knew that was wrong, but she had no other way of reading the smudged word.

Nastimania went into the ladies cloakroom and became Queen Lilywhite. She stumbled out onto the station platform, approached the shoebox and its contents, tried to stand on her tippy-toes (but she kept falling over), closed her eyes, raised the magic wand above her head, forgot what she was going to say, and cried: "RAMKATLAMMETJIE!"

Bonk! There was a puff of smoke and a flash of lightning followed by a thick cloud of smoke and dust. There on the railway line stood an old, rusty, beaten-up tugboat with smoke coming out of the funnel. An old sea captain (Fungus the frog) was leaning over the bridge smoking a pipe and the sailors (Greaseball, Meatball and Furball) were all running around trying to catch a batch of honking purple penguins.

The people of Franchhoek streamed to the station to see this strange sight. When Kosie Koekemoer and Sterling Mustard arrived at the station to board the Blue Train for Pretoria and saw what had happened, they headed for the national highway to the North.

Queen Lilywhite was last seen heading for the woods with a half-empty champagne bottle in her hand. An old man leaning crookedly on his walking stick on the platform of the Franchhoek station was heard to mutter, "I came out here today especially to see the pong go."

Unfortunately all the King's horses and all the King's men (and the pong) would be spending (at least) another day in Franschhoek.

And to this very day soldiers in the Army are referred to as Pongos.

12

The Tokolossies

South Africa is very much like any other place in the World. We're just a little bit behind everything that happens elsewhere. When everyone else had TV, we had camp fires (and they're still known as the TV of the Bushveld). When everyone else had motorcars, we had ox wagons. When the world was watching movies, we were watching sunsets. But we think that we have the one thing that no one else in the world has. We have the Tokolossie.

The correct African word is *tokoloshe,* which is a gremlin by the way, but we just say Tokolossie. So, what is a Tokolossie? Well, it is a small man with big feet, pointed ears, a scraggly beard on the end of his chin and a tail like a monkey. He is a pesky little fellow that always gets up to mischief. In fact, he does a lot of damage when he starts to play tricks around your home or your farm. When the milk goes sour, it's the Tokolossie. When the porridge gets burnt, it's the Tokolossie. When the cock crows at two o'clock in the morning, it's the Tokolossie. When the cookies disappear from the cookie jar, it's the Tokolossie. When the doorbell rings and you go to open the door to find that no one is there, it's the Tokolossie.

The African people in South Africa are very frightened of the Tokolossie. They believe that he can kidnap people and make them do things that they would never normally do. That is why, in most African homes, the people place a number of bricks under each foot of their bed so that the Tokolossie cannot reach them. But why all this stuff about the Tokolossie? Well, this story is about the day that Yeti and his friends met up with the Tokolossie during the Great TREK.

It was raining in the veld. Yeti loved the rain, because where he came from the rain turned to snow – and he just loved the snow. Jak and Dodgy, however, were wet and miserable.

"We have to find a dry place where we can rest," grumbled Jak as they plodded across the veld with the rain running down his neck.

"Yes," agreed Dodgy, "a nice dry place with a warm shower and a soft bed and a table full of lovely food and a fireplace to keep us warm and some nice woollen slippers for our sore feet and ..."

"**Barnacles!**" said Yeti. "This is perfect weather for travelling and we have to keep travelling if we want to win this TREK."

Just at that moment, out of the gloom, they came upon a little grass hut called a *rondawel* in South Africa. It was round, with a thatched roof and there appeared to be a small fire burning inside. When you're big and strong and smelly and wet you can probably walk in anywhere without first knocking. Yeti walked straight in.

"Hello! Is anyone home?" called Jak politely.

"Do you see anyone in here?" asked Yeti. "The place is empty."

"Why is this bed standing on bricks?" asked Dodgy, pointing to an empty bed neatly made up with sheets, blankets and pillows.

Jak gave a big sigh. He knew why the bed was standing on bricks, but did not really want to tell Yeti and Dodgy because he did not believe in the Tokolossie. He told them anyway.

Dodgy immediately jumped onto the bed. Yeti had a good laugh. "We've also got little men like that where I come from," he said. "We call them goblins."

As the three friends sat around the fire in the little rondawel, Yeti told Jak about the goblins. They only come out at night, bang on the pots and pans in the kitchen and, when the people get up to see what all the noise is about, the goblins rush into the bedroom and pour water into the bed or pull all the bedclothes off.

"The best way to deal with goblins," explained Yeti "is to pull their hat over their eyes so that they can't see. Then they run around bumping and banging into furniture and walls and doors as they try to get home."

"What are you doing in my house?" There in the door of the rondawel stood a man with a big fat belly dressed in the uniform of a policeman. Well, under his dripping raincoat he was dressed in the uniform of a policeman. He had bushy eyebrows and a shaggy moustache and was clearly annoyed. But when Yeti stood up and stretched to his full height the policeman was no longer annoyed.

Jak politely explained to the policeman that they had come into his rondawel to get out of the rain. They would leave the moment it stopped raining. Till then they would like to share his dry rondawel and his warm fire. The policeman looked at Yeti again and immediately invited them to stay as long as they wished. He then introduced himself.

"My name is Kerneels. Kerneels van der Merwe. Constable Kerneels van der Merwe of the S A P S. I am the Tokolossie policeman around here."

He went on to explain that he had been living in the veld for ten years trying to do this job, but that he had never caught a single Tokolossie.

"Now I have another job," he said. "I got a letter in the post today. My Headquarters has told me to start looking for three suspects that tried to blow up the whole of Kimberley with dynamite."

Yeti looked at Jak. Jak looked at Dodgy. Dodgy looked at Yeti. Then they all looked at the policeman.

"What are you going to do if you catch these suspects?" asked Jak.

"I've been told to take them to a coal mine where they can work underground until they've paid for the damage they caused," said Constable Kerneels.

Jak looked at Yeti. He knew what Yeti was thinking. There was no way that this tubby policeman would ever get Yeti to go underground to work in a coal mine.

"Why is your bed standing on bricks?" asked Jak, just to change the subject.

The policeman pulled his neck down into his shoulders, looking around as if something or someone was sneaking up on him. His knees shook and his tummy wobbled. "Oh, I just like sleeping high above the ground," he said with a nervous little giggle.

But we know the truth, don't we? The policeman was afraid of the Tokolossie.

It was still raining heavily. Constable Kerneels invited Jak and Yeti and Dodgy to spend the night in his warm, dry rondawel. He offered them each a Klipdrif (brandy) and Coke for a nightcap but, as you know, our friends never drank any *dop,* so they had a glass of warm milk instead.

Soon they were all comfortable, our friends around the fire and Constable Kerneels in his tall bed. Jak and Yeti and Dodgy lay awake, just waiting for Constable Kerneels to fall asleep. Soon he was snoring loudly.

"Go and fetch some more bricks," said Yeti. Jak and Dodgy rushed out into the rain. They found a huge pile of bricks around the back, bricks that Kerneels had bought to extend his rondawel. Soon the whole pile of wet bricks was inside the rondawel. Yeti gently lifted the bed with the sleeping policeman in it. Carefully Jak and Dodgy added bricks to the columns under each foot of the bed. Then Yeti carefully placed the bed back on the bricks. The bed reached up to the ceiling of the rondawel where it swayed gently just like a tall tower of Lego bricks.

"Let's get out of here," whispered Yeti. "There's no way I'm going to work in a coal mine. It will take this fat policeman all day to get off his bed without crashing down. Then he has to take all those bricks outside again. By that time we'll be far, far away." Quickly and quietly they each put on their raincoat, shouldered their rucksack and slipped out into the night.

As they plodded through the mud on that wet and stormy night Jak thought that he heard chattering and giggling and shuffling behind them. Soon Yeti and Dodgy heard the same weird noises. They all stopped behind the trunk of a large tree, waiting to see what was following them. Out of the misty night came a whole tribe of little men with large feet, pointed ears, scraggly beards at the end of their chin and each with a tail like a monkey.

"**Boo**!" cried Yeti in a loud voice, jumping out from behind the tree, hoping to frighten the little men away.

"Ha, ha, ha," they laughed. "We knew you were going to do that," said their leader. "We're Tokolossies and we know everything."

"We want you to be a Tokolossie too," said the smallest of the gang. "We've been trying to get rid of that policeman for ten years, but we can't get at him because his bed is too high. Won't you join us and become an "Honorary African Tokolossie"? Think of all the fun we could have."

"I'm not a small little man," said Yeti crossly. "I may have big feet, but I don't have pointy ears or a beard or a tail like a monkey."

"We can change all that," said the Tokolossie leader. "We'll put a magic spell on you so that you look just like us."

"What if I don't want to?" asked Yeti, puffing out his chest. "What are you going to do about that?"

"Well," said the littlest Tokolossie, "we'll just follow you around for the rest of your life and play tricks on you wherever you go. We'll make your life miserable."

Jak walked up to Yeti and motioned him to bend down so that he could whisper in his ear. Then Yeti stood up straight again, as tall and stout as a wild oak tree.

"All right," said Yeti, "I agree to become an Honorary African Tokolossie, but I want to stay as big and as tall as I am now. I want to be known as the Biggest, Tallest Tokolossie in the World."

The Tokolossies made a big bonfire in the middle of the veld in preparation for the ceremony (it had stopped raining by now). Everyone stood around the fire with the flames dancing on their face and in their eyes. In the darkness beyond the fire were the bright, shining eyes of the many wild animals that had come to see what all the fuss was about. There were antelopes, hyenas, jackals, *blouwildebeeste* (gnus), lions, rhinoceroses and many other beasts.

"Please turn your backs," said Yeti in what he thought was a good impression of a solemn Tokolossie voice. "I want to get dressed in my best ceremonial suit."

The Tokolossies all politely turned their back to the fire. Suddenly, out of the blue (out of the black, really, but you know what I mean) there was a great commotion. Yeti was stamping on the fire with his extra-large feet. Suddenly it was pitch black again. Oh, my soul! There was smoke and dust everywhere. There was screaming. There was cursing. There was tumbling and struggling. There was laughing and roaring and grunting and raging. In the commotion and the confusion our three friends slipped away into the night.

What the devil had happened? Well, when Jak whispered in Yeti's ear he told him the secret of getting rid of Tokolossies. You simply have to get them to turn their back and then tie all their tails in a knot. The Tokolossies can't reach behind them to untie the knot. Magic! It's almost the same thing as pulling Goblin's hats down over their eyes.

The rhinoceroses, who were watching all this unfold, had also learned a valuable lesson from Yeti. To this very day, whenever there is an untended fire in the veld, you may be sure that a rhinoceros will come charging over to stamp it out with his big feet.

Long after the sun had come up over the fresh, sweet-smelling plains there were still ghostly sounds of laughter in the quiet African morning. The jackals and the hyenas were still chuckling and giggling at the plight of the Tokolossies. It is a uniquely African sound that can be heard every morning, but you have to be out of doors on the quiet African veld to hear it.

13

The Kruger Millions

Note to young readers

Before continuing with this saga, it might be a good idea to give you a brief lesson in South African history, just to help you understand the story, and the significance, of the Kruger Millions.

At the turn of the Century (that was when 1900 became 1901), some one-hundred-and-a-handful of years ago, there was a country in the very heart of the Bushveld called the South African Republic. It later became known as the Transvaal, which means on the other side of the Vaal River. The President of this Republic was Oom (meaning 'uncle') Paul Kruger.

Even though he was President, which is very much like a King, Oom Paul was just an ordinary farmer. There are many stories told about this man, some of them true and some of them just plain lies. For example, it is said that Oom Paul never wore socks in his life. He grew up with the popular *velskoene,* simple home-made shoes of untanned leather, which are very comfortable when worn without socks. So even today in South Africa, when men walk around in shoes without socks, we say that they are wearing "Paul Kruger nylons."

Paul Kruger went to England once, to meet Queen Victoria in London. Oom Paul, who didn't smoke but chewed tobacco, had the bad habit of spitting tobacco juice wherever he went. It was said that he was so good at spitting that he could hit a fly at five paces. Anyway, in the Queen's palace, spitting on the floor and on the carpets was really not the thing to do. In those days, in the bars where the men went for a *dop,* there were shiny round brass pots for people to spit into. They were called "spittoons." In Buckingham Palace in London, where the Queen lived, the spittoons were made of gold – but there they were called "cuspidors".

One day, while Oom Paul was having tea with the Queen, he kept spitting on a most beautiful Persian carpet. One of the Queen's servants, called a Footman, brought a gold cuspidor and placed it next to Oom

Paul's chair. So Oom Paul spat on the carpet on the other side. The Footman again moved the cuspidor to where Oom Paul had last spat. Oom Paul promptly spat onto the carpet where the cuspidor had just been removed. He then called the Footman over and whispered to him, "Listen *Boet* (son), if you keep moving that pot around, just now I'm going to spit in it." I am inclined to believe this story.

At the State Banquet to welcome Oom Paul to England, he was surrounded by Princes and Princesses, Dukes and Duchesses, Knights and Ladies, all of them trying to make a good impression on the Queen. Everyone knew that the Queen loved poetry. In order to please the Queen, certain gentlemen at the table were making clever little rhymes like:

Your Highness Divine,
Please pass me the wine.

Or:

Your Highness, 'tis my wish,
May I please have more fish?

Well, Oom Paul thought that he would show the Queen, and the clever Englishmen, that he too could make a charming little rhyme to amuse the ladies. So, when the coffee was served, he said,

"Johannes, jou bogger
Please pass me the sogger."

(Or, in English, 'John, you bugger please pass me the sugar'.)

This is one story that I am inclined not to believe. But allow me tell you a true story about this man that you may read in a history book called "The Lost Trails of the Transvaal" by the author, TV Bulpin.

One day Oom Paul went hunting for rhinoceros. He was far from home when he finally tracked down the animal he was looking for. While he was loading his gun with black powder and a ball, the musket exploded and Oom Paul severely injured his left thumb. The thumb was treated with what medicine they had and bandaged up. Unfortunately the wound festered and became a serious problem. Oom Paul was concerned that he would get blood poisoning or something equally serious. He did not want to have his arm amputated, or cut off, as a result of his wound so he promptly cut off his thumb with his pocket-knife. The wound took many months to heal, but he did not lose his arm.

When Oom Paul was President, gold was discovered on the Ridge of White Water in the Transvaal (the *Witwatersrand* in Afrikaans). There was a gold-rush in South Africa and miners came from all over the world to make their fortune. When they realised that South Africa probably had the most productive and extensive gold mines in the world, Queen Victoria and her advisors decided to take the South African Republic from Oom Paul Kruger and his people. Kings and Queens think they can do that sort of thing, but it led to war between the British and the South African Republic.

The British and the *boere* (farmers) fought for many months, until it became clear that Queen Victoria's army was going to win. Oom Paul and his government fled from Pretoria on the railway line that led to the coast in Mozambique, to the City of Lourenço Marques. They took with them all the government's money in gold coins that were worth one pound each. These were known as Kruger Pounds.

Oom Paul fled to Holland and to Switzerland, where he died of old age. He died a poor man, so everyone wondered what had happened to the fortune that he had taken from Pretoria when he fled. People that had fought in the war, on both sides, started spreading the story that Oom Paul had hidden the treasure somewhere between Pretoria and Lourenço Marques. That is how the legend of the Kruger Millions was born.

The day after Yeti had tied the tails of the Tokolossies together, he and his friends were sitting on the *stoep* (veranda) of a farmhouse on the banks of the

Vaal River. The farmer, old Oom Bertus van der Merwe, lived and worked all alone in the house and on his farm. He was a widower (ask your Mom or Dad what that means) and all three his sons had left the farm to join the Police Force. So, Oom Bertus was very pleased to have company and invited Yeti, Jak and Dodgy to stay with him for a few days. He told them all about being a farmer in the Transvaal and also about prospecting for gold when he was a young man. Then he told them about the Kruger Millions. He told them that his grandfather had fought for Oom Paul Kruger against the British. He had also been part of the escort that went with the President to Mozambique when they all fled from Pretoria.

"I have something that I want to show you," said Oom Bertus.

The old man stood up, went into the house and returned with a large book covered in black leather.

"This is our family Bible," he said as he sat down in his rickety old rocking chair. "Look at this. This was written in my grandfather's own hand."

The scrap of paper that he handed to Jak was old, torn and yellow with age. The ink was faded, but Jak could still make out the words that were written in a thin scrawl, almost like the trail of an ant that had walked across the page. Jak read the note to Yeti and Dodgy. This is what it said:

"There was an old man without a thumb
Who fled with a pot of gold.
He hid it in a mountain cave,
Or so the story's told.
If you want to find the pot-o'-gold
Just follow the nose on your face.
But use your Head and not your heart
To discover this special place."

"Now look at the back," said Oom Bertus.

Jak turned the scrap of paper over and saw a faded drawing with squiggles and arrows and a small cross.

"Well, what do you think of that?" asked Oom Bertus.

"Not much," replied Dodgy. "It's just a rhyme and doesn't even give us a clue where to look for the pot of gold. That drawing on the back means nothing if we don't know where to start."

"OK," said the old farmer, "if you're not interested I'll just put the Bible back in my study."

"No, no, wait!" said Jak. "Maybe we can take that scrap of paper and go and look for the gold. May we have it?" he asked politely.

"Well, I was going to give it to one of my sons," said Oom Bertus, "but they're clearly not interested. Would you like to buy it from me?"

"We don't have any money," explained Yeti, "but we could do some work here on the farm for you. Would that satisfy you?"

The old farmer looked around at his farmyard. "Look at this place," he said sadly as he pointed to the rubbish in his yard. "It's littered with old tyres, broken down tractors, old truck wrecks, broken machinery, a windmill that has fallen down and all sorts of other scrap. One barn door is broken right off, the vegetable garden is overgrown with weeds, and that little building that serves as my dairy has not been painted in years. The roof of the stable has collapsed and the chicken coop is just a pile of rotting poles and rusty wire."

Yeti was suddenly very sorry that he had offered to do some work on the farm.

"If you could sort out this mess, the treasure map on the scrap of paper is yours," said Oom Bertus with a deep sigh.

Yeti, Jak and Dodgy sprang to work. After two hours of sweating and straining they had made no impression whatsoever on the untidy farmyard. Three more hours of dragging and stacking and burning and building saw a slight improvement. Another three hours later Oom Bertus stood on the stoep of his house and beamed down at the three friends as they lay sprawled on the lawn, which had just been mowed. The farmyard was transformed.

"I didn't remember the old place being so big," said the smiling farmer as he surveyed his neat yard with its painted dairy, repaired stable, the new barn door and the rebuilt chicken coop. With a flourish he handed the old scrap of paper to Jak.

"You've earned it," he said with a tear in his eye, for he knew that he would be alone again the following day.

Sunrise the next day saw Jak, Yeti and Dodgy walking briskly across the veld in the direction of Lourenço Marques.

"Why are we going to Lourenço Marques?" asked Dodgy.

"We went there for a holiday once," replied Jak. "It's a beautiful place with lovely beaches, warm water and nice people. And the food is fantastic."

"Then we shouldn't be looking there for the gold," said Yeti. "The rhyme says that we should use our head and not our heart in our search. And, by the way, Lourenço Marques is now called Maputo."

"But if the food is fantastic, maybe it's the best place to start looking," said Dodgy as his tummy gave a loud rumble.

"I agree with Yeti," said Jak, "but where should we start looking?"

"Let's have a look at the map," replied Yeti "Maybe that will give us a clue."

So they all sat down in the shade of an umbrella thorn tree and studied the map. The part that they were really interested in was the area between Pretoria and Lourenço Marques.

Suddenly Jak jumped up and started bouncing up and down like a rubber ball. "I have it! I have it!" he cried. "I know where to look for the gold."

Yeti got Jak to calm down and to explain exactly what he meant.

"Look," said Jak, producing the scrap of paper from his pocket, "Yeti is right, the note says, 'Use your head'. Here on the map the only place between Pretoria and the border that uses the word 'head' in its name is Graskop. Graskop in English is Grass Head. That is where we have to go to find the gold … in a cave near Graskop".

It did not take long (about six days) before Jak, Yeti and Dodgy were walking down the main road of the little town of Graskop. Many, many years ago it was at the centre of a gold-rush in the district. Today, however, it is a small town that provides goods and services for the local farmers and hotel accommodation for tourists. As they walked along, Jak spotted a small tea-room in the centre of the small town.

"Look at that," he said, pointing at the little shop. He took the scrap of paper from his pocket. "The name of that place is "The Pot-o'-Gold". Let's go in there and make some enquiries."

Jak, Yeti and Dodgy walked into the tea-room, sat down and looked around. The old photos on the wall were all taken during the great gold-rush, when the town of Graskop was booming. In the middle of the wall, above the fireplace, was a photo of Oom Paul Kruger and his advisors during the war against Britain. Just then a pretty young lady came up to take their order.

"Do you know anything about the Kruger Millions?" asked Jak.

"Of course I do," she replied. "This is Graskop. Every year we have crazy people from all over the world that spend weeks in the bush searching for the hidden treasure."

Jak ordered a Coke, Yeti ordered a cup of tea and Dodgy ordered muffins, pancakes and a waffle with cream and syrup. And a bucket of water and a bale of hay.

"I'll tell you a secret," said the pretty girl with a smile. "Some time ago we printed a little rhyme on small scraps of specially-prepared paper. We sent the scraps of paper to friends all over South Africa and asked them to spread them around. On the paper we printed a little rhyme about a hidden treasure, making as though it was a riddle linked to the Kruger Millions. We even made a little drawing on the back, with squiggles, arrows and a small cross, creating the impression of a treasure map. The idea was to encourage people to solve the riddle – then come to Graskop, but more particularly to our little tea-room. Did you notice our name?"

Jak took the scrap of paper from his pocket.

"Yes", said the girl, "that's one of our little rhymes with the map on the back. Wherever did you get it?"

Yeti started laughing. He laughed and he laughed until the tears streamed down his face.

"We've been tricked," said Yeti between more great gusts of laughter as he saw the sheepish look on Jak's face.

"What do you mean, we've been tricked?" asked Dodgy grumpily.

"Read that scrap of paper carefully. There are two parts to the rhyme, and they have no connection. The first part tells us about a man without a thumb, OK? The second part tells us how to find the pot-'o-gold. Well, we've found the Pot-o'-Gold! That sneaky old farmer on the Vaal River got us to do a day's work for him, and then sent us here to Graskop for a cup of tea."

The sounds of laughter spilled from the Pot-o'-Gold into the sunny streets of Graskop. Far away, on the banks of the Vaal River, an old farmer sat in his rocking chair on the stoep, wondering why his ears were tingling.

14

The Muddy River

Sterling Mustard and Kosie Koekemoer were racing across the Karoo, where there is very little water, but were very careful not to kick up too much dust. Yeti (and friends) had been on TV a number of times for making too much dust in the Karoo. Sterling and Kosie did NOT want to spend a night in jail. They had not seen Mac, the mechanic, for some time and needed to fill up with gas, or petrol as they had learned to call it in South Africa. Suddenly it started raining.

"Oh no," groaned Kosie. "Mac will never find us in this downpour, so we'll have to find a dry place to sleep for the night. Your car's tank is almost empty, so we can't go too far."

They drove along carefully on the slippery, muddy road. At times they had to stop for goats, or donkeys or a flock of sheep on the road. The shepherds were nowhere to be seen, probably sheltering in a leaky rondawel or grass hut somewhere. The rain continued to fall in a solid sheet. Suddenly they came upon a gate across the road.

"We're lost. Again," said Kosie glumly. "Nobody builds a gate across a public road. We must be on someone's farm. Again," he added, with a sigh.

"Look," said Sterling. "There's a sign by the gate. What does it say?"

"It says, "Welcome to Seekoeivlei."

"What's that?"

"It's probably the name of the farm. A *seekoei* is a hippopotamus and a *vlei* is a swamp. Please don't tell me we're driving into a swamp."

Kosie got out of the car, opened the gate and allowed Sterling to drive through. He got back into the car, dripping from top to toe. Sterling shuddered when he saw all the mud on his car's carpets from Kosie's boots. Sterling moved forward slowly. He could hardly see the road in front of him. It was getting dark and the rain was not helping matters at all. All of a sudden they came to a dead stop.

"Why are you stopping?" asked Kosie.

"Because we're stuck," mumbled Sterling as he tried reversing out of the mud.

The more the car moved backwards and forwards the deeper it sank into the mud. At last the racing car's belly was resting on the mud, with its wheels spinning wildly.
"That's done it," said Sterling with a sigh. "This is as far as we go."

There they sat, in the mud, with the rain pouring down and not more than ten drops of petrol in the tank. What a mess!

Then, out of the gloom and through the pouring rain, appeared a battered and muddy farm bakkie. Out of the bakkie jumped a tall, wiry man in shorts and a short-sleeved shirt. He had a floppy khaki hat on his head and velskoene, with Paul Kruger nylons, on his feet. (Do you remember what "Paul Kruger nylons" are?) Without a word the man secured a chain to the towing hook on the racing car and pulled them out of the mud with his bakkie. Before Kosie could get out of the car to say "thank you" the man drove off. They could do nothing but ride along behind the bakkie with wave after wave of thick mud being thrown onto the windshield from the bakkie's wheels.

"I'll never, ever get my car clean again," moaned Sterling as it became caked in the sticky wet mud.

Then, just as suddenly as it had started raining, the rain stopped. Kosie and Sterling couldn't see a thing as the windows were all covered in mud. Then they heard the man unhook the chain from the car, they heard the bakkie drive away and they heard a scraping sound followed by a loud clang. It sounded like a large metal sliding-door that had been shut.

Kosie and Sterling got out of the car. To their great surprise they saw that they were inside a large barn with other tractors, trailers and an old pick-up truck standing on wooden blocks, wheels in the air, in the corner.

"Dit reën lekker daarbuite, nê?" said the old truck, "maar dit lyk vir my jy het in die vlei vasgeval."

"What is that rusty old truck saying?" asked Sterling as he tried to get his car's wipers to move the mud from the windscreen.

"You can call me Blikkies," replied the old truck in a thick Afrikaans accent (and bad grammar). "I are saying you fell fast in the vlei. You outlander townies should be more careful driving around the veld in the rain, you could bedonnner your car's smart paint job."

The farm tractors in the barn hooted and rumbled with laughter.

"Die karretjie lyk of 'n koei op hom geskyt het," (the car looks as if a cow has crapped on it) said a big John Deere tractor and the tin roof of the barn rattled as the laughing went from loud to crazy, drowning out the sound of the rain. Silence fell at the sound of the barn door opening. The young man that had towed Kosie and Sterling from the mud drove in with his bakkie. He got out of the bakkie, dripping water and mud onto the concrete floor of the barn. He set up a small table, then laid out a feast of cold lamb, bread, butter, cheese, fruit, a jug of milk and a thermos flask of rooibos tea. He then carried a sack full of firewood to a fireplace against the stone wall and soon had a blazing fire going. He unloaded two folding camp-beds from the bakkie, then placed rolled-up sleeping bags on the beds. In all this time the young man did not speak a single word. With a cheerful wave he got back into his bakkie and drove out of the barn, closing the sliding door behind him.

"Well," said Kosie, "that's the nicest fellow that never spoke to me."

"Dit was Kleinkosie," said Blikkies from his corner. "Kleinkosie Vannermerwe. He are the farmer around here. He always wanted to be a policeman but he are deaf and mute, so now he are a farmer. He may not talk much but he are the finest farmer innie distrik."

Kosie and Sterling helped themselves to the most delicious supper they had tasted in a long time. Kosie added more wood to the fire, Sterling switched off the bright fluorescent lights in the barn and they crawled into the sleeping bags. The tractors and the old truck were creaking and cracking contentedly as the fire warmed their chilly parts. It was not long before the sound of snoring was competing with the sound of the rain on the tin roof.

The next morning dawned darkly, windily and wetly. It was still raining. Shortly after dawn, Kleinkosie drove into the barn and placed a steaming three-legged pot of *mieliepap* (maize-meal porridge) and a jug of milk on the table. While Kosie and Sterling were having breakfast, Kleinkosie took Sterling's car out into the yard where he filled the tank with petrol. He also gave the car a good cleaning with the high-pressure water hose, using steaming hot water to get rid of the sticky mud. As Kleinkosie drove the car back into the barn the tractors looked at it with new respect. They had never seen such a smart-looking racing-car before.

Kleinkosie then went back into the barn, put a jack under the old pick-up truck, removed the wooden blocks and placed the old truck on its wheels. He then filled the old truck with petrol, checked the oil and water and inflated the tyres.

"Hier kom 'n ding," (now something is going to happen) old Blikkies rumbled as Kleinkosie started the engine.

After breakfast Kleinkosie attached a chain from the old truck to the front tow hook of the racing-car.

"Good luck!" roared the farm tractors as they drove out of the barn.

It was still pouring with rain as Blikkies towed Kosie and Sterling across the muddy veld. There was no sign of the farm road, but Kleinkosie seemed to know where they were heading. Blikkies drove slowly and carefully, so there was not a lot of mud splashing over Sterling's car as they made their way to … who knows where?

They had been driving for about twenty minutes when the old truck stopped. Before them was a raging torrent of water, clearly a large river.

"Where are we?" asked Sterling.

"Nee, ek weetie," replied Blikkies. "I was never off this farm, so I only know where I are on the farm. We call this river the Muddy River."

"Why is the water so red?" asked Sterling.

"Aha, I know where we are," replied Kosie. "The water is red-brown from all the soil that is washed down into the river by the rain. That is called soil erosion and this is the Orange River, so called because of the colour of the mud in the water. This is the biggest river in South Africa."

"OK, so how are we going to get across?" asked Sterling.

"Moenie worry nie," ("no worries") responded Blikkies, "I often cross this river on the old ferry. Kleinkosie will take you across then bring the ferry back again. He does it every week when he goes to town to fetch the post and to buy groceries. If we have to cross the river at the bridge, we need to drive a hundred miles and it takes a whole day to get to town and back. When we use the ferry we take a short-cut and it takes about three hours."

Kleinkosie walked down to the water's edge where a sturdy ferry was bobbing, securely tied to a large willow tree. There was a hard-packed gravel ramp leading to the ferry, a clear indication that it was in regular use. Kleinkosie motioned for Sterling to drive his car onto the ferry, which he did. Soon the car was securely fastened to the deck with strong straps. Sterling felt quite comfortable on the ferry and was happy that the pelting rain was washing away the last traces of the horrid mud from his car.

The ferry, built to take one vehicle at a time, was attached to an overhead cable that ran from one side of the river to the other. The cable was anchored to large concrete blocks sunk into the ground on either side of the river. The ferry was driven by a strong outboard motor that appeared to be in very good condition.

When everyone was on board, Kleinkosie indicated that he was ready to cast off. That means that he was ready to start the outboard motor, untie the ropes and prepare to cross the river. From the bank of the river Blikkies the old truck winked cheerfully at them with his one good headlamp. Kosie took a deep breath, Sterling gave a merry wave, and Kleinkosie untied the rope allowing the ferry to drift off into the fast-flowing current.

A new adventure was about to begin.

15

The South African Ark

It was still raining, in fact it was pouring. The rolling, bubbling torrent of muddy water raged down the Orange River in the direction of the sea. Every now and then, a big chunk of the riverbank tumbled into the raging river, while old rotting tree trunks and even whole trees drifted past in the strong current.

"I've never been on a ferry before," said Sterling as Kleinkosie Vannermerwe slowly edged the bulky craft away from the bank and into the main stream of the river.

"Don't worry," said Kosie Koekemoer as he patted the racing car's bonnet. "I'm sure he's done this hundreds of times before."

Kleinkosie saw the concern on their faces and gave his two passengers a confident "thumbs up" and a big wink from beneath his dripping khaki hat.

The overhead cable took the strain of the ferry and the outboard motor chugged away powerfully as they moved to the centre of the river. Then, out of the pouring rain, appeared a huge willow tree. Twisting and tumbling in the raging water it was headed straight towards the ferry. Before Kosie could even give a warning cry the tree struck the ferry right in the centre, its whippy wet branches and long leaves suddenly cascading all over Kosie and Sterling like some crazy green octopus. Suddenly they all heard a loud crack. The overhead cable, unable to take the strain of both the ferry and the huge tree, had snapped.

The ferry lurched to one side and Kosie was almost swept overboard. Fortunately the rails along the side of the ferry prevented him from falling into the raging water. Kleinkosie quickly checked the straps securing Sterling's car to the deck and gave thumbs up. The ferry spun even further around, dragged along by the drifting willow tree. Then, with a jerk, the tree was free and drifting away on its own. The sudden turn had plunged the outboard motor under the water. It stopped running. Kleinkosie hurried to the spare motor to get it started, but it had been knocked off its mountings by the willow tree and had disappeared overboard into the swirling water. The ferry was tossing and turning helplessly as it was swept downstream.

"Look!" cried Kosie, pointing to a monkey in the water with another tiny monkey clinging to its back. Kleinkosie saw the plight of the monkeys and quickly tossed a length of the mooring rope in their direction. The mother monkey grabbed the rope and was soon hauled aboard the ferry. The moment her feet touched the deck she scrambled under the car to get some shelter from the pouring rain. They heard her chattering away as she did her best to calm her terrified baby.

Kosie looked across the deck and saw Kleinkosie leaning far into the water, trying to grab hold of a long wooden plank floating by. Soon the plank, which looked like a floor plank from some derelict old house, was on board. The farmer cut up a length of rope with his pocketknife and lashed the long plank to the rear of the ferry with the longest piece hanging overboard into the water.

"Why, that's brilliant," said Sterling. "Now we have a rudder and we can steer this boat."

All they could really do was steer the ferry away from serious trouble ahead. There was no way that they could prevent the ferry from being swept downstream in the raging current.

Then Kosie saw a donkey in the water. It was trying desperately to reach the riverbank, but the current was too strong. Kleinkosie signalled to Kosie and Sterling that he was going to steer in the donkey's direction. Kosie used hand signals from the front of the ferry to give the direction in which he should steer. In a flash they were right on top of the donkey. Kleinkosie left the rudder for a moment, leaned over the edge of the ferry and grabbed the donkey by its ear. The ferry, without the rudder, started turning in the water. Kleinkosie waited until the ferry was downstream of the donkey, then used the push of the river to try to haul the donkey aboard. The donkey did its best to help by scrambling with its front legs and kicking powerfully in the water with its back legs. With a final huge effort, assisted by Sterling, Kleinkosie finally dragged the donkey safely onto the deck.

The next animal they came across was a pig, then a chicken, then a porcupine. All were safely hauled aboard the ferry as it continued its journey towards the sea. As they travelled in a Westerly direction, they saw many other rivers and streams that were adding their water to that of the Orange River. More trees and more animals were encountered. They hauled a small herd of five sheep aboard, then some bedraggled goats. Another donkey. A calf. A young horse.

"Look at this," said Kosie.

The deck was covered with beetles and bugs, worms and spiders, snails and slugs, ladybirds and grasshoppers. The insects had managed to cling onto the ferry as it passed them thrashing about in the raging river and then to climb to the safety of the deck. An owl, perched precariously in the branches of a tree in the middle of the river, lifted off and flapped its way bravely through the rain to land on the racing car's roof. Two bedraggled yellow-billed ducks soon joined the owl.

"Yuck!" said Sterling as the first drop of guano was deposited on his car's roof.

On and on they went, mile after mile in the Orange River that had burst its banks. And as the ferry made its way helplessly towards the sea, more and more birds and animals and insects managed to find refuge on the ferry's deck. The new passengers included a badger, a jackal, a young springbok ram, another pig, more chickens, two snakes and a very old sheepdog. The deck of the ferry was cluttered with all these unplanned passengers, all of them just thankful that they were out of danger.

Out of danger? Well, not quite!

"We have a problem, Sterling," said Kosie to his friend. "Kleinkosie may not know it, but this river has a huge big waterfall somewhere up ahead. They're called the Augrabies Falls. The next big town that we will pass by is called Upington. Shortly after that we'll be head-over-heels over the Augrabies Falls – if we're not careful."

"I think you'd better warn the farmer," said Sterling. "If we can't get off this river the ferry will surely plunge over the waterfall and we'll all be lost."

Kosie went across to where Kleinkosie was steering the ferry with the improvised rudder. From his shirt pocket he took a soggy notebook and a stub of pencil and tried to make a drawing of a waterfall. His drawing must have been pretty good because Kleinkosie was soon nodding his head vigorously. Kleinkosie then made signs showing that the river would become very wide up ahead. He also pointed to the heavens and indicated that the rain would soon stop falling. Kosie understood what he was trying to say. If it stopped raining there would be less water flowing into the river and if the river became wider it would also become calmer. It was clear that Kleinkosie had given the problem a lot of thought.

Suddenly Kleinkosie pointed to something up ahead. It was a deserted farmhouse with water up to the windowsills. They had seen many such buildings along the river as they drifted by, but in this case there was a clothesline with sheets, towels, shirts, pants, socks and other clothes hanging out in the rain. Kleinkosie pointed at his dripping clothes and signed to Kosie and Sterling that they should grab some of the clothes from the clothesline as they passed by. Kosie and Sterling stood at the front of the ferry while Kleinkosie leaned over the side at the back. As they swept past the clothesline they all extended their arms and grabbed all the clothes that they could reach. There they stood, each with an armful of wet clothes.

"So, what do we do now?" asked Kosie.

Sterling shifted into the front seat of his car, started the engine and turned the car's heater to full blast. Then he squeezed as much water as possible from the wet clothes and draped them all over the seats. He closed the car's door. The air-conditioning would do the rest. As this was done, they sighted the outskirts of Upington. Soon after that the river would begin to broaden and become calmer. They would have to act pretty soon, for the Augrabies Falls were not very far away either.

Kleinkosie motioned to Kosie to take over the steering, which he did. The young farmer then motioned to Sterling and the two of them went to the outboard motor to see if they could start it. They tried on a number of occasions, without success. They tried again. Nothing happened. Then the practical farmer and the racing driver sat down and took the motor apart. It was the first real opportunity that they had to do so. They took all the parts and laid them out on the carpet in front of the car's passenger seat. Sterling took a handkerchief from the seat, which by now was fairly dry, and carefully wiped off each part making sure that it was clean and dry.

"We'd better do something quickly," shouted Kosie from his position at the rudder. "We're in the calm water already and I can hear the waterfall up ahead."

Kleinkosie could, of course, not hear a thing. He and Sterling took their time assembling the motor, making sure that no moisture would prevent it from starting. They placed the motor back onto its mountings and were busy securing the bolts when the ferry lurched violently to one side. They had struck a rock. Kleinkosie looked up and saw Kosie pointing up ahead. There, not more than a few kilometres ahead, they saw the mist rising up into the sky as the raging waters plunged over the waterfall.

When Kleinkosie looked back at Kosie again there was a big smile on his face. It was his turn to point. Kosie and Sterling turned around to see what Kleinkosie was pointing at. It was a brilliant, perfect rainbow with all its colours showing up beautifully against the dark clouds; violet, indigo, blue, green, yellow, orange and red. Then they noticed that something else had changed. It had stopped raining.

Kleinkosie turned his attention back to the motor. He gave the starting rope a strong tug. Nothing happened. He tugged again. Again nothing happened. He tried a third time. With a cough and a splutter and a little cloud of blue smoke, the motor started. At that very moment the ferry rounded a bend in the river and there, up ahead, were the thundering, deadly Augrabies Falls. Kleinkosie gave a twist to the accelerator of the motor. The motor responded, working perfectly. Sterling then engaged the gear to get the propeller turning. The ferry responded immediately. Kleinkosie pointed at the nearest bank of the river and Kosie swung the rudder over to move in that direction. Kleinkosie gave the motor more power and, for the first time since the ferry's cable had snapped, they were in full control again. With a great whoop of triumph and joy Kosie steered the ferry, and all her passengers, to safety.

At the riverbank, Kosie rammed the front end of the ferry up into the mud. Sterling and Kleinkosie jumped off and secured the mooring rope to a large blue gum tree. When they got back on board, Kosie was taking off his wet clothes and replacing them with dry clothes from the inside of the car, the clothes they had grabbed from the clothesline. The clothes did not fit very well, but at least they were dry. Kleinkosie and Sterling wanted to do the same, but could find no clothes to fit. At last, in desperation, Sterling put on a lady's nightdress that was meant for a *boere-tannie* (farmer's wife) several sizes larger than he was. He tightened his belt around his waist, tucked in the nightdress as best he could, and was comfortable at last in dry clothes. He hung his sodden hat over the railings to dry out and took a dry towel, wrapping it around his head and down the back of his neck like an Arab.

Kleinkosie draped a long striped tablecloth across his shoulders and through his legs, knotting the ends around his waist. He then wound a dishcloth around his head for protection from the sun. Then Sterling, Kleinkosie and Kosie started carrying all the animals off the ferry, placing them back on the land for the first time in three days. The animals and the insects, all still confused by the rain and the flood, did not immediately run away. The goats and the sheep and the chickens and the donkeys and the pig had become quite accustomed to the presence of Sterling, Kosie and the farmer, so they stood around feeding in the grass close to the ferry. The sun came out from behind the clouds and beamed down on the small group of survivors of the big flood standing under the arch of a perfect, beautiful rainbow.

Frikkie September had lived beside the Orange River all his life. He was eight years old. His father and mother worked on a grape and wine farm and they all lived in a pretty white house on a rise overlooking the mighty river. He had never seen such a flood before and was happy when, at last, the rain stopped and he could go down to the river to see what was happening. He was walking barefoot through the sticky, yucky mud when suddenly he turned and ran straight back home.

"Come look, Ma, come look!" he shouted as he raced into the kitchen where his mom was baking bread. "Come quickly," he said, grabbing his mom's hand and dragging her outside towards the river. "Come and see, Ma! There's a bible story happening down by the river, right here in front of our house."

16

The King is Not Amused

A lion roared. **"I've had enough of this nonsense!"** The great big roar came out of the very heart of the Bushveld. Leaves fell off the trees, birds flew up into the air with fright and small animals scurried off, with their tail between their legs, to find their mommies. Louis the Bushveld Lion was clearly upset about something, but what? Did he have a sore tooth? Was his tail caught in a thorn bush? Did he have a bellyache? There was silence in the Bushveld as all the animals, minding their own business, found a nice quiet spot where they could keep out of the way of the grumpy old Lion King.

"Where is that stupid owl? **Where is he**?" The next great roar echoed across the quiet veld and was heard by the Wise Old Owl as he sat high up in the shade of a Camelthorn tree having his morning nap. Squirt the squirrel came bounding up the tree trunk.

"The King is looking for you, Owl," he said breathlessly. "Can't you hear him calling?"

"Shouldn't you be collecting nuts?" asked the old owl through the side of his clenched beak as he frowned at the little squirrel.

"The worst possible time to go and see a lion is while he is in such a foul temper. I'll wait for him to calm down and ***then*** I'll go and see what's bothering him."

A moment later the old owl, leaning against the tree trunk, was snoring gently.

Well, as the Wise Old Owl had predicted, things did calm down in the Bushveld. Louis was feeling much better after a big lunch and a nice long snooze. Even the pesky flies buzzing around his ears, his moustache and his nose did not appear to bother him. He only opened his eyes and lifted his majestic head from the soft sand when he heard a calm, deep voice addressing him.

"Good afternoon, Your Majesty. I believe you have been calling for me? How may I be of service?"

The Wise Old Owl sat on a low branch just out of reach of the lion. He knew that it is better to be safe than sorry, as you never can tell how a grumpy old lion will react when waking up after a nap.

The Lion King sat up slowly and gave a majestic flick of his tail, sending the flies in all directions. He squinted into the setting sun, trying to focus on the owl that was almost invisible where he sat amongst the leaves with the sun behind his back.

"It's this Great TREK thing," the Lion King grumbled. "It started months ago and there is no end in sight. Those kids and their crazy guests are running around South Africa causing nothing but trouble. If they're not frightening the animals, they're creating great clouds of dust. Or they're floating all over our skies in balloons and steaming around the country in a smart new Blue Train. Or they're getting involved in tribal conflict and they're even blowing up our mining industry. They're forever getting lost or searching for treasure or floating around our rivers on a ferry. When does it all end?"

The owl listened to Louis complaining about the Great TREK. He was quiet for a long time. The Lion King thought that the old bird had fallen asleep again.

"Ahem." The Wise Old Owl cleared his throat. "Your Majesty," he said in his diplomatic voice. "The purpose of the Great TREK was to celebrate your 40th birthday, to bring visitors to South Africa and to show the World what a wonderful place this is. Our visitors have been on the TV almost every day since they arrived. Now, if our visitors make cake dry (this is a direct translation of an old Afrikaans expression that means you're 'making a fool of yourself') then it is ***they*** that should be embarrassed. The important thing is that South Africa is seen on TV for the wonderful place that it is. I think, Sire, that we are getting excellent international publicity."

"Well, if you say so." The Lion King rolled onto his back and lay in the cool sand with his paws flopped over and with a silly grin on his face, like a puppy.

"I'm bored," he said, to no one in particular. "I want this TREK to be completed so that I can hand out the prizes. I think the animals want to see a lion on the TV for a change. They want to see, well, **me**."

"Yes, Your Majesty. I'll see to it right away."

"And, Owl," said Louis as he sat up and shook his dusty mane, "find something for me to do. Something important. And do it soon! You don't want to end up as a feather duster in some tacky souvenir shop in the Kruger National Park, do you?"

"Certainly not, Your Majesty," said the owl calmly. "Certainly not!"

But, expecting to be treated with disrespect, the owl had come prepared for his meeting with the cranky old Lion King. He had a trick up his sleeve. (Not that owls wear shirts with sleeves, but you know what I mean).

"Feather duster, nogal!" he muttered grouchily under his breath.

In his left claw the Wise Old Owl was holding the very tip of the very long tail of a very agitated *veldmuis* (field mouse). He had caught this particular mouse near the hyena's den, a den renowned throughout the Bushveld for its horrid, nasty, pesky fleas. The owl took off from the low branch and, on his silent wings, flew right past the rear end and bushy tail of the lion ... where he dropped the wriggling mouse with its terrible cargo of terrible fleas.

"I'm sure something will turn up to keep you busy for the next few days, Sire," called the Wise Old Owl over his shoulder as he flew off into the sunset.

That night the drums could be heard from the north to the south, from the east to the west. **Doem-doem, doem-doem, doem-doem, doem.** On and on it went, way beyond midnight. The deep, thumping notes of the drums throbbed and echoed across the Bushveld, flitting through the forests, marching across marshes and galloping over the grasslands. The sound skipped from koppie to koppie and floated across the rivers as the message of the drums boomed its way into villages, towns and cities across the country. As one warrior completed the drumming sequence, another would repeat it, spreading the drummed message all over, like the ripples in a pond when you throw a stone into the water.

Yeti, Jak and Dodgy were sitting on the top of a little hill outside Pretoria watching the sunset.

"What was all that banging about last night?" asked Dodgy.

"Those were African drums," replied Jak. "That is how the Africans talk to one another instead of using telephones."

"But then everyone can listen to your conversation," remarked Yeti.

"That's the whole idea," said Jak. "The messages that are sent are for everyone to hear, like the death of an important person or the birth of a Chief's son or an invitation to a wedding."

"Does everyone understand the message of the drums?" asked Yeti.

"No," replied Jak, "and especially not the young people. But every village has a wise old man who explains to those that do not understand. If the message of the drums is meant for you, somehow you'll get it."

"Excuse me for disturbing you, young man," came a deep voice out of the gloom. Standing behind them, facing the setting sun with a strong face and deep, dark eyes, was an old man with an animal-skin cloak around his shoulders and a long walking staff in his one hand, an envelope in the other.

"Are you Jak of the Bushveld?" he asked politely.

"Yes I am, Baba," said Jak, politely using the African expression "my father" to address the elderly man.

The old man bowed slightly, handed Jak the envelope, turned and disappeared into the gathering gloom.

Jak took a box of matches and a stub of candle from his leather pouch. He opened the envelope and, by the light of the candle, he read the note inside:

Louis the Lion King wants you to get a move on.

No date, no address, no signature.

The next day at a small little railway station called Hessie se Water, in the middle of the Free State, the Blue Train was busy loading up some more of the King's horses and the King's men. They had landed there by balloon many weeks before and were only too pleased to be getting out of the dry and dusty Free State. Young Bobby Breen and Dorothy Dunbar were standing on the platform stretching their legs and looking out across the rolling plains when they were approached by a *piekanien*, a small African child, carrying two envelopes.

"Are you Bobby Breen and Dorothy Dunbar?" asked the young boy politely.

"Yes!" replied Bobby.

"My grandpa sent me to give this to you." The young boy handed an envelope to each of the children, turned, walked to the end of the platform and disappeared. They both opened their envelope and read the note inside. The notes were identical.

Louis the Lion King wants you to get a move on.

No date, no address, no signature.

Kosie Koekemoer and Sterling Mustard were pulling into a service station in Marydale on their way back to Bloemfontein after their adventure on the ferry. A wrinkled old attendant with hardly any teeth in his mouth filled the car with petrol.

"Are you Kosie Koekemoer?" he asked.

"Yes," said Kosie.

When the old man handed Kosie his change for the petrol, he also handed him an envelope, which Kosie opened in order to read the note inside.

Louis the Lion King wants you to get a move on.

No date, no address, no signature.

Animals and birds, like the Wise Old Owl, may not be able to write and they can't use telephones and cell phones, but they know how to get their message across, don't they?

The Wise Old Owl flew across the Bushveld to a little *pannetjie* (a small pond) that still had some muddy water left in it from the last rains. All the animals knew where it was, but on this particular day there was only one animal using it – the Lion King. The old owl landed on top of an anthill beside the pond and watched in amazement as the lion rolled around in the sticky, yucky, smelly mud.

"**Ahem**!" The old owl got the lion's attention.

The bedraggled, filthy, smelly Lion King sat in the middle of the pond wiping mud from his eyes.

"Your message has been delivered to all the contestants, Your Majesty. The Great TREK will be terminated within a few weeks," said the owl in his solemn advisor's voice.

The Lion King stuck his head into the mud.

"Must you do that, Sire?" asked the Owl irritably as he watched the lion wriggle and squirm in the mud like a baby elephant, splashing some of the sticky stuff against the anthill that the owl was perched upon, some of which splashed onto his immaculate flea-free feathered feet.

"Oh yes, oh yes," murmured the muddy lion happily. "This feels soooooo good. This is the first time this week that I've not been tortured by those horrid, pesky fleas. If it weren't for you they would have driven me mad by now. Thank you **ever** so much for telling me that a mud bath is the only sure way to get rid of fleas."

"You're welcome, Your Majesty," said the Wise Old Owl, bowing his head solemnly as one does in the Court of a King. "That's what friends are for."

17

Preparing for the End of the TREK

—

You're not going to believe this, but the Blue Train and its load of King's Horses and King's Men eventually arrived in Bloemfontein. Jak put Bobby Breen in touch with Lieutenant Pearce, Jak's Uncle Eddie, at the Parachute Battalion. They arranged for Humpty Dumpty to move into the Officer's Mess, but he was warned not to go anywhere near the kitchen … probably because soldiers just love scrambled eggs.

The King's horses and the King's men were promptly moved to the military base, on the outskirts of the town. The people of Bloemfontein very quickly started calling this camp TEMPE, which stands for **T**emporary **E**ncampment for **M**ilitary **P**ersonnel and **E**quipment. Although there was an airfield nearby, the camp was built especially for Pongos. Remember, where the Army goes, the pong goes.

Kosie Koekemoer, Sterling Mustard and Mac with his truck had also rolled into town. Mac was tired of chasing all over the country trying to locate Sterling, who was forever getting lost in the farming district or getting caught in a flood and drifting down a river to the sea. Mac's bum was sore and his truck was in urgent need of a service and an oil change.

That evening, over a *braai* (a South African BBQ) in the garden, Bobby Breen, Dorothy Dunbar and Kosie Koekemoer got together for a serious discussion.

"Did you guys hear all those crazy drums booming out across the veld about a week ago?" asked Kosie.

Dorothy and Bobby both nodded.

"And the next day, did you receive a strange note?" asked Kosie. "One without a date, an address or a signature?"

Dorothy and Bobby both nodded.

"Well, we'd better get a move on," said Kosie. "I hear that the Lion King get angry very quickly. My dad says he has a very short fuse. We don't want him to get angry and cancel the Great TREK before we've even completed it."

"OK, so how are we going to do this thing," asked Bobby. "If I allow the British Ambassador to get involved again, all the King's horses and all the King's men are going to be spread all over the country, like the last time. It will take us weeks to get re-organised again."

"I agree," said Dorothy. "And I'll do my best to keep my crazy Queen away from any party or wine-tasting."

"And I've got to get my speed-freak friend to stick to the national roads for a change. And to avoid speeding," was Kosie's rueful contribution.

Over the *pap-en-sous* (grits and meat-sauce), *tjops* and *wors* (lamb cutlets and sausage) the three young contestants hatched what they thought was a great plan. They would load all the King's horses and all the King's men onto the Blue Train. The train would take them to the border town of Messina, less than 100 kilometres from the farm Last Penny, the final destination. They would then march from Messina up to the Limpopo River to complete the Great TREK.

It was late and the three children were still excitedly discussing this plan, when there was a phone call for Bobby. When he returned he had a very long face.

"Bad news," he said. "That was the Stationmaster. He called to tell me that the Blue Train has disappeared into thin air. What are we going to do now?"

Queen Lilywhite and Prince Bandilegs were standing in the shadows listening to this conversation.

It had just turned midnight. That was why the Blue Train had so mysteriously disappeared, remember? The not-so-hot magic wand, right? And, what's more, the cheap-and-nasty magic wand could only do the same trick for a maximum of ten times before it jammed. No more Blue Trains from that sticky stick, Nastimania knew.

So, Bandilegs was no longer a Prince, but had turned back into Fungus the frog. Lilywhite was no longer a Queen, but had become Nastimania again, with her hooked nose, broken teeth, green eyes and bad breath. And no more Blue Trains. It made her head spin. She decided that she would go to bed, sleep on the problem and hopefully come up with a solution by the next morning.

The next morning, bright and early, Queen Lilywhite walked into the kitchen where Bobby Breen, Kosie Koekemoer and Dorothy Dunbar were having breakfast.

"Why so glum, everyone?" she asked cheerfully as she flounced in with her crown at a cocky angle on her head.

Dorothy explained that there was not much time left to complete the Great TREK and that there was a major problem in moving all the King's horses and all the King's men up to the Limpopo River in time.

"Hmmm," said Lilywhite as she stood with her arms folded and her right index finger on her chin. "I think I have a solution."

"Don't even think about the Blue Train," said Bobby. "That has disappeared into thin air. And we can't march the horses and the men all the way up North. That would take ages, and we don't have the time."

"Look," said Queen Lilywhite, "it's Humpty-Dumpty that is the VIP. All the King's horses and all the King's men are only the military escort for the fat egg. If we get him there safely, the problem is solved. All we need is one horse and one man to represent the other horses and the other men and to make the VIP look good. Ask me. I know. I'm a Queen."

"That sounds great," said Dorothy, "but how are we going to get them to the Limpopo River?"

"I know, I know," said Kosie excitedly. "I will drive up North with Sterling Mustard, and this time we'll stick to the highway. Mac can drive behind us with his transporter. As Mac will not be transporting the racing car, there will be plenty of space in the back of the truck. Dorothy can drive up front to make sure that Mac does not get lost and Bobby, Queen Lilywhite, Prince Bandilegs, Humpty-Dumpty, one horse and one man can travel in the rear."

Well, well," said Queen Lilywhite smiling at Kosie, "aren't you the clever little travel agent."

She was just itching to whip out her magic wand and turn Kosie into a bug deflector to mount on the racing car's bonnet.

Actually, she was very pleased, as that had been her plan all along. All she had to do was to ensure that everyone was safely in bed every night by midnight so that they would not see a beautiful, sophisticated Queen turn back into an ugly, bedraggled old hag. These were thoughts that she kept to herself, however. Wouldn't you?

Once the plan was accepted, everyone got to work to make it happen. Mac's truck got its long-overdue service and oil change. Sterling's racing car was given a special wash, wax, polish and shine. The many new small cracks in Humpty-Dumpty's shell were carefully patched with vinegar and brown paper and carefully painted over. Nastimania packed her shoebox neatly and wiped the dust from her magic wand. The three boys packed their rucksacks with clean underwear, socks, a toothbrush and a set of smart clothes for the big party to celebrate the end of the TREK. Then Bobby Breen went over to TEMPE to select the King's horse and the King's man to be Humpty-Dumpty's escort.

The first thing that Bobby did when he spoke to the soldiers was to ask for volunteers. Big mistake! Why? Well, the very first thing that you learn when you are a soldier is never to volunteer. That is because the Sergeants always play nasty tricks on the soldiers that volunteer. Let me give you some examples:

- The Sergeant asks for volunteers that can play musical instruments. Then he gets the volunteers to carry a piano from one place to another.
- The Sergeant asks for volunteers that have driving licences. Then he gets the volunteers to each "drive" a broom around the parade ground, sweeping it from end to end.
- The Sergeant asks for volunteers that are interested in art. Then he gets the volunteers to paint the guardroom.

So, naturally, Bobby got no volunteers. The next problem was to decide which horse and which man to send.

"Leave this to me," said Lieutenant Pearce, Jak's Uncle Eddie. "I know how to deal with stubborn soldiers."

The paratrooper spoke to all the King's Men and told them that there would be an inspection to decide who would go with Humpty-Dumpty as his escort. This would be an inspection with a difference, however. He would not select the smartest soldier with the smartest horse, but the sloppiest soldier with the untidiest horse. Then everyone would help to get the sloppy soldier and slipshod horse up to scratch to be Humpty-Dumpty's escort.

"No one wants to be selected as the sloppiest soldier on parade," Eddie explained to Bobby, "so everyone is going to do his best to be the ***smartest*** soldier on parade. Then, at the last minute, we change the rules of the inspection and select the smartest horse and the smartest soldier. It's called reversed psychology."

The soldiers were given 24 hours (that's a whole day) to prepare for the inspection. Eddie was right; no one wanted to be known as the sloppiest soldier, so they sprang to work. They washed and cleaned and polished and ironed and starched and rubbed and scrubbed. It was going to be the finest inspection that TEMPE had ever seen.

Bloemfontein is not a very large town, so it is very difficult to keep a secret there. That is why everyone knows that Grey College is the best boys school in the whole wide world. So, within the hour everyone knew about the big inspection that was to be held at the military base. The next day there were hundreds, no thousands, of people standing around the parade ground to watch the inspection. After all, it's much better than sitting in your car by the side of the highway watching other cars pass by.

At eight o'clock on the dot the band started playing and all the King's Horses and all the King's Men marched forward. There was clapping and cheering and loud shouts of appreciation as they marched onto the parade ground for the inspection.

It took a long, long time to find the smartest horse and soldier because they were all perfect. All day long they stood on parade while Lieutenant Pearce and Bobby Breen marched up and down looking at their boots and their buttons and their buckles and their saddles and their bridles and all the other stuff that makes horses and soldiers look so smart. Eventually a decision was made, the best horse and the smartest soldier were selected and the crowd gave three cheers for the winners.

Twenty minutes later everyone was loaded into the back of Mac's truck, with Humpty-Dumpty safely seated on a pile of mattresses, surrounded by soft pillows. The crowd shouted "BON VOYAGE" while Queen Lilywhite waved regally from the open back of the truck (until it pulled away suddenly and her crown toppled over her eyes and she was heard to make a remark that cannot be repeated in this children's story).

Kosie Koekemoer and Sterling Mustard led the way out of Bloemfontein, to the wild cheering and clapping of a huge crowd, on the final leg of the Great TREK.

18

Rushing to Get the Job Done

Jak was sitting in his underpants with his back to a thorn tree, his clothes hanging out to dry over several bushes close by. Dodgy was lying on his back in the sun, steam rising from his tummy, his legs straight up in the air, his head to one side with a big grin on his face. Yeti was also lying on his back, with his hands behind his head. He was lying in a puddle of water with a frog sitting on his tummy watching him. The three friends had been caught in a bushveld thunderstorm. When the first loud claps of thunder rang out and the lightning bolts flashed across the veld, Yeti and Dodgy had whimpered and cowered like chickens in a hailstorm. They were astonished when Jak removed his clothes and started hopping and jumping around in the rain.

"What is the matter with this boertjie?" muttered Dodgy as he curled up in a wet ball with his hoofs over his ears. "Boertjie" was one of many words he had picked up on his travels. It means "little farmer".

Yeti, as you know is dressed all in white. When he is frightened, which is not very often, his face turns a sort of pale purple and his eyes get bigger and bigger. The lightning struck an old tree nearby and there was a strong smell of sulphur in the air. Yeti's eyes were like saucers and he had turned a bright purple with yellow blotches. They could not believe that Jak was running around like a fool with his arms spread wide, splashing through the mud like an earth-bound swallow.

"Come on!" shouted Jak above the thunder, "Come and join me!"

The two citizens of the Kingdom of Shangri-La had never seen such a storm before. They were terrified.

Jak stopped his whooping and jumping for a moment. He went across, grabbed Yeti by the hand and Dodgy by the ear, dragging them into a small clearing.

"When I was a little boy I was also afraid of the thunder and lightning," he said. "Then one day my grandpa took me by the hand, took me outside in a thunderstorm and taught me just how exciting and wonderful it can be. Then he said something that I will never forget. He said, 'Don't be afraid of the storm.

Learn to dance in the rain.' So, come on, let's dance in the rain."

So, the three friends danced in the rain. They splashed and hopped and whooped and swooped. The other animals that saw this strange behaviour just shook their head and turned their back against the wind and rain. Yeti and Dodgy, however, were no longer afraid.

After a while the thunder calmed down, the wind dropped, the lightning stopped and the pouring rain became a light drizzle. The storm was moving off to the eastern horizon. The clouds broke and the sun shone through. That is when Jak hung his clothes out to dry and sat down against the thorn tree, Dodgy lay drying out in the sun and Yeti lay back in a cool puddle of water with a new friend.

"This is nice," said Jak as he stood up and stretched, reaching up into the air as high as he could, "but it's getting us nowhere. We have to do something about finishing this Great TREK."

"You're right," responded Yeti. "Louis the Bushveld Lion is not going to be satisfied if we don't get a move on. When Kings give instructions they expect them to be obeyed. Ask me, I know."

"So, what are we going to do?" asked Dodgy. "There's no wind around here, so a sailing soapbox car won't work. It will take ages if we try to walk all the way. What are we going to do?"

"I know, I know," said Jak excitedly. "Do you remember when we were in the coffee shop in Graskop? What was its name?"

"The Pot-o'-Gold," replied Yeti with a smile as he remembered how they had been hoodwinked by that crafty old farmer.

"Yes, that's right," said Jak. "Well, there I saw a photo of some of Paul Kruger's soldiers on a bicycle that was built to run on a railway line. It was actually a contraption made of two tandem bikes built onto railway carriage wheels. So, the machine can carry four people and, instead of pedalling on the road, the bicycle runs on the railway tracks."

"Aha!" said Dodgy. "So we can get on the bike and pedal all the way to the border. What a brilliant idea!" Dodgy was already thinking of a nice gentle ride on the bike watching the game along the way while Yeti did all the work.

Jak, Yeti and Dodgy were soon on their way to the closest railway line, which happened to be at the little station of Hammanskraal, north of Pretoria. That night, at around midnight, they ran into two fellows pushing their bikes along, on the way home after an evening of celebration at the local tavern. Yeti met them in the middle of the road, hoping to convince them to sell their bikes to him. Well, these two chaps didn't wait around to have a long conversation or to haggle about the price with a huge white giant with big feet. They dropped their bikes right there in the middle of the road and were last seen heading for the high ground at great speed, getting rid of their tekkies (tennis shoes) as they pulled away. As they ran off into the dark, one was heard to mutter something to the effect that, "This is the last time that I drink the rubbish that old Sally brews in her miserable shebeen." (Ask your mom … no, on second thoughts; ask your dad what a 'shebeen' is. If he doesn't know, surprise him by telling him that it's a place where illegal alcoholic beverages are brewed).

The next morning our friends found four rusty old railway wheels abandoned by the side of the track. Soon the bikes were mounted on the wheels with their chains attached to the axles and it was not long before Jak, Yeti and Dodgy were pedalling merrily along in the direction of the northern border.

Going uphill was a bit of a problem, but Yeti had powerful legs and they would soon be over the hump and on the way down the other side. Everything was going just fine until they hit a long, steep downhill slope. It was then that they discovered that their contraption had no brakes.

It all started off as a welcome break from the hard work of pedalling uphill. As they crested the little hill, it was a relief to sit back and enjoy the free ride down the other side. The gentle breeze on their face was pleasant as it cooled the sweat on their brow. Then the slope got steeper and the breeze increased to a strong flow of air. This soon turned into a powerful wind as they hurtled downhill.

"Not so fast!" shouted Dodgy, whose ears were no longer flapping in the wind but blowing straight back like two furry wings.

"Hang on and sit still," called Jak as he grabbed hold of his hat before it was swept off his head. "This thing has no brakes and we don't want to go off the rails at this speed."

Faster and faster they went, rushing downhill like an express train with the wheels humming on the tracks. The telephone poles were flashing past in a blur and the wind was whipping tears from Jak's eyes. Faster and faster, ever faster. Then they all heard a faint tinkle in the background of the rushing wind. The tinkling became louder and louder. Then they heard a voice crying faintly in the wind.

"Hey! You! Stop!" it called. "Stop, I say. Stop in the name of the law!"

There was nothing they could do, so Jak, Yeti and Dodgy clung grimly to the handlebars of their bikes. The shouting behind them had stopped, but the tinkling continued without abate. Eventually the steep hill levelled off until there was a long piece of straight, flat track ahead of them. Their vehicle moved slower and slower until the whole contraption came to a halt, the wheels still red hot from the downhill charge.

Jak, Yeti and Dodgy heaved a sigh of relief before turning around to see what, or who, had been following them in the thrilling descent. Behind them they saw a man in a uniform of short blue pants, a blue shirt, long blue socks and black shoes dismounting from what looked like a very strange bicycle. Well, it looked like an ordinary bicycle, but it had no tyres. Instead, the tyres had been removed and the rims of the wheels flattened so that the bicycle could run on a single railway track. The man rang his bicycle bell, which gave the tinkling sound that they had been hearing for the last half an hour. He removed a crumpled cap from his pocket and jammed it on top of his head. He removed a pencil and a notebook from his shirt pocket, hitched up his pants and came walking over.

"Good morning," he said, "my name is Pikkie. Constable Pikkie van der Merwe of the S A P S. Who is in charge of this vehicle?"

Jak, Yeti and Dodgy groaned. They knew what was coming, but this was the last place in South Africa that they had expected to be caught for speeding.

The policeman spent some time taking down all the details. He was not very friendly and Jak could just imagine having to spend some time at the police station while the matter was sorted out. Then Jak had a good idea. He asked Constable van der Merwe if he had heard all that drumming during the night a few days ago. The policeman nodded. Then Jak took that strange note from his pocket and showed it to Pikkie. The policeman read the note.

Louis the Lion King wants you to get a move on.

"Oh my soul!" he said. "I know this guy. I tried to give him a ticket once. Not for speeding, but for lying down in the middle of the road and obstructing the normal traffic flow. It took me three days to get out of the *wag-'n-bietjie* bush (a thorn bush that grasps, holds and punctures anyone and anything that touches it) when he was done with me. I even had to buy a new uniform. A week later I found my cap in some lion manure on my front lawn. I know this guy *en hy vattie kakkie* (takes no nonsense). If he hears that I held you up for a speeding ticket, there will be really ***big*** marrakas and I don't have money for a new uniform and a new hat."

Later that afternoon the animals along the railway line heading up to the border saw a very strange sight. There was a policeman riding his bicycle on a railway track, ringing the bell as he rode. Behind him was a strange contraption with a young boy and a great big white, furry monster-looking creature pedalling furiously. Behind the white giant was a goat seated on the carrier with a smile on his face, his front legs folded, his back legs on the handlebars and his ears and tail trailing along gently in the breeze.

The Wise Old Owl was sitting in a tree beside the railway track. He watched as Constable Pikkie, Jak, Yeti and Dodgy pedalled along, sweat dripping from their faces (all except Dodgy's … of course).

The Owl flew off sedately on silent wings. The mysterious letter was having the desired effect. It was time to make preparations for the celebrations to mark the end of the Great TREK.

19

The End is Nigh

The Wise Old Owl was pulling feathers from his head, but only because owls have no hair. He was frustrated, he was annoyed and he had a problem that he just could not resolve. Problem? Indeed! The King of the Beasts had told him to arrange a grand party to celebrate the end of the Great TREK – but nobody could tell him when the TREK was going to end.

Louis (the Bushveld Lion and the King of the Beasts, remember?) wanted a band. Then he changed his mind; he wanted an orchestra instead. He told the Owl that they should have a fancy-dress party. Then he changed his mind because he realised that all the animals were **already** in fancy dress. His final demand was for the Owl to arrange an awards ceremony, with a red carpet and prizes for each contestant, just like they do at the Oscars ceremony in Hollywood. He wanted all his guests to see the Bushveld at its very best and he wanted them to go back home and tell the world what a wonderful place it was. But he still wanted an orchestra. The Old Owl was just waiting for the King to call him and to change his mind again. Now you know why he was pulling the feathers from his head.

The Wise Old Owl flew around the Bushveld looking for an orchestra. Everybody told him that the field mice had the best orchestra of all, but he could not find them anywhere. He got directions from the mossies (sparrows), but when he arrived at the spot there was not a mouse in sight. As he landed on a branch all he could see were long mouse-tails disappearing into the bush. He wondered why.

The Owl flew over to the local *watergat* (watering hole) where he hoped to find an animal that knew about other orchestras in the Bushveld. A muddy warthog with bushy eyebrows told him about some creatures calling themselves **The Crickets** that had been playing together for some time, but he didn't think they were very good. The Owl said nothing, but had his own thoughts on the level of music appreciation to be expected from warthogs. A shy little *stokstertmeerkat* told the Owl about a group that called themselves *Die Sonbesies* (The Cicadas) that were apparently quite the rage at the moment. A hornbill told him that he had heard of a whole family of *toktokkies* (black beetles) playing together, but they were apparently more interested in drumming than in real music. An Impala ewe was about to say something regarding a choir of frogs when she saw that the Owl was no longer there. No one had heard him fly off into the shimmering bush, plucking out feathers as he went.

If the Wise Old Owl only knew what further problems were waiting for him, he would have continued flying until he reached a nice quiet spot where no one knew him and where concerts and orchestras and award shows never, ever happened ... like Alaska or Siberia or Outer-Mongolia.

Fortunately he knew nothing about the future and went along enthusiastically making plans for the Great TREK Award Ceremony. **Un**-fortunately he had to include the Bushveld animals in his plans, and that is where all his problems lay.

Bushveld animals, like most other inhabitants of South Africa, are proud, stubborn, often argumentative, and generally very bright. They have inflated egos, plenty of self-confidence and lots of aggression. The Wise Old Owl knew all this, yet he made plans to include many of the animals in his upcoming pageant. He needed waiters and ushers and barmen and security guards and hat-check girls. He needed cooks and cleaners and gardeners and ticket collectors. In fact he needed the entire population of the Bushveld to help him lay on the Big Bash.

Then he discovered that he couldn't use the lions and leopards and hyenas for security guards because they would probably eat the guests. He also found that crocodiles make terrible chefs because they eat all the food that they prepare. Rhinos are useless at looking after hats and coats because they always fall asleep and forget where they have put the stuff. Impalas make terrible gardeners because they eat all the grass and flowers. Elephants make too much dust, the buffaloes frighten away the guests, people keep tripping over the warthogs and monkeys just want to play. But worst of all; no one ever turns up for training or rehearsals. It was a total disaster.

At that stage the animals gave the Wise Old Owl a nickname; Kojak. (Entertainment Note for those too young to remember. Kojak (played by the actor Telly Savalas) was a famous American TV detective, very popular in South Africa, with **not a single hair on his head**.)

Just as things were at their worst, and Kojak was seen walking around with a squint singing a lullaby that his Mom had taught him when he was a chick, the gang from Bloemfontein rolled into the Bushveld in a cloud of dust. Kosie Koekemoer and Sterling Mustard were leading the way. Right behind them came Mac in his truck with Bobby Breen riding up front in the cab. In the back were Dorothy Dunbar, Queen Lilywhite, Prince Bandilegs and Humpty-Dumpty with a King's horse and a King's man as his escort. Sterling had to slam on the brakes to avoid running over the Wise Old Owl. Mac also slammed on his brakes to avoid smashing into the back of Sterling's car. In the back of the truck Humpty-Dumpty banged his head against the metal sides and everyone was really concerned that his shell had cracked, again, as a streak of yellow was seen running down his chin.

Queen Lilywhite jumped out of the truck to give someone a considerable piece of her mind, her magic wand ever ready to turn the offender into a flea or a carrot or whatever. When she saw the little old owl lying in the dust with not a feather on his head she immediately summed up the situation. She needed no introduction; she instantly recognised the Owl as a VIP and knew that he must be attached to the court of the King in some way. Maybe he was in charge of protocol, or foreign visitors – maybe even the arrangements for the End of TREK Party. She was very worried about the Old Owl's condition and just knew that she had arrived in the nick of time. Only she, Nastimania, er, Queen Lilywhite, could save the day. She gently picked up the old bird, wrapped his thin and trembling body in her royal cloak and was last seen making for a nice shady spot under a camelthorn tree.

At that very moment Jak, Yeti and Dodgy came marching up the road from Messina singing, *"We are Marching to Pretoria"* (while marching in the wrong direction). They had arrived on their strange railway contraption a few hours earlier and were walking the last few kilometres to the farm Last Penny, then on to the Limpopo River where the Great TREK would finally end.

There were wonderful scenes of celebration as all the contestants of the Great TREK got together again. They made camp right there beside the road, they built a cosy campfire and were soon swapping stories, gasping, laughing and crying at all the adventures that they had experienced.

The friends sat around the campfire talking until late into the night. Then someone started yawning, which set all the others off to yawning too, and they all got up to crawl into their sleeping bags for a well-earned rest. Prince Bandilegs just made it into the shadows before turning into a frog. No one had seen Queen Lilywhite since before sunset, but throughout the night sounds of a serious discussion, interspersed with giggles, could be heard coming from the shadows under a big old camelthorn tree. The talking and giggling continued until dawn.

The next morning everyone awoke to the most amazing sights. There were long tables laden with a fine breakfast and a whole team of warthog waiters to serve everyone. All the contestants had a good breakfast before dressing in their finest party clothes. They decided that they would all walk down to the Limpopo River together and to arrive at the end of the Great TREK at exactly the same time. They would all be the Winners.

There was no sign of the dusty old farm road. Instead there was a smooth paved road covered in rose petals. On both sides of the road were white stones marking the way from the campsite all the way down to the river. According to plan, everyone joined hands and walked the final stage down to the river together. Sterling followed in his car with Humpty-Dumpty sitting comfortably on a stack of cushions, his shell neatly patched up with vinegar and brown paper. Then came the King's horse and the King's man followed by Mac and his truck. The whole procession moved down towards the river, cheered on by hordes of Bushveld animals that had come to see the spectacle.

On the banks of the river was an open-air theatre with a big stage and plenty of comfortable seats for the contestants and the invited guests. There were flags and banners and ribbons everywhere and more long tables creaking under the weight of the finest food, all in the shade of large, airy tents. An orchestra of furry animals dressed in tailcoats was playing the most beautiful music. In the background a large choir, the Sparrows and Larks, were warming up for their performance. Smart soldiers in their best uniforms surrounded the whole venue. The Bushveld looked absolutely magnificent. Kojak (the Wise Old Owl) and Queen Lilywhite were, however, nowhere to be seen.

The Bushveld animals crowded around the stage, everyone pushing and shoving, trying to find the best spot to see the show. The contestants and invited guests were ushered to their seats by smiling antelopes while the orchestra played quietly in the background. Then the orchestra stopped playing and silence fell across the veld. Suddenly there was a loud fanfare of trumpets and Louis the Bushveld Lion, the King of the Beasts in his splendid cloak with a golden crown on his head, came striding onto the stage. Queen Lilywhite, wearing her finest robes and a diamond tiara, followed him out carrying the Wise Old Owl on her left wrist. The King sat down on his throne, flanked by two of the tallest soldiers. Queen Lilywhite walked to the centre of the stage where she stopped. The silence was complete; you could have heard a tiny composite leaf fall from a thorn tree. The Wise Old Owl cleared his throat before declaring in a strong, clear voice that carried across the Bushveld,

"My name is not Kojak!"

20

The Great TREK Awards Ceremony

There was total silence in the crowd … until the owl's stunning statement echoed back from the surrounding acacia and baobab trees.

"My name is not Kojak!"

The Bushveld erupted and was swept by gales of laughter. In an instant the Lion King was on his feet. He swept his royal cloak back across his shoulders, thrusting out his broad, muscular chest. Silence fell as the assembled animals dropped their heads. With his piercing yellow eyes sweeping across the multitude, looking for any sign of discord, the King said in a quiet, menacing voice, "The. Wise. Old. Owl. Is. My. Most. Loyal. And. Respected. Councillor." He paused for effect. " Just look at this magnificent pageant he has laid on for your pleasure. If ***anyone*** ever calls him Kojak again, that animal will be banned from my Kingdom … ***forever***!"

"Wow!" said Yeti under his breath. "This guy really is a King!"

All the other visitors were too frightened to say a word. The Lion King stood for a moment longer, staring out menacingly across the crowd, before turning to Queen Lilywhite who was still holding the Wise Old Owl on her wrist, her knees quaking with fright.

"You may continue with the Awards Ceremony, Owl," he said, and the King returned to his throne.

Two soldiers marched on and placed a tall silver perch right in the centre of the stage. Queen Lilywhite gently placed the Owl on the perch before walking calmly, if a little wobbly, to her seat with the other contestants.

"Ahem!" The Owl cleared his throat.

Then, one by one, he introduced each contestant in the Great TREK to the audience, inviting them to join him on the stage. There were great cheers from different parts of the theatre as a favourite contestant appeared. The turtles and the ostriches loved Humpty-Dumpty, whistling and stamping their feet as he waddled onto the stage. The frogs cheered wildly when Prince Bandilegs was introduced. This really puzzled the Lion King, but we know why, don't we? The rabbits went crazy as Sterling Mustard revved his car's engine, drove up the special ramp and parked in the centre of the stage, right beside the Wise Old Owl. Dodgy was greeted by loud squeals of delight from all the goats and antelopes, but everyone stood up and cheered loudly when Yeti was introduced. He had become known as the "gentle giant" during his stay in South Africa and everyone knew about his regular brushes with the law. From his humble origins in the high mountains he had risen even higher to become a popular leader in his own Kingdom and was seen as a sort of a "go-between" for humans and monsters.

When the applause eventually died down Kosie Koekemoer, Bobby Breen and Dorothy Dunbar all received polite applause as they walked onto the stage, but there was another standing ovation as Jak appeared. Everybody in the Bushveld knew about Jak and his deep love of the veld. It was on his dad's farm, Last Penny, that the ceremony was taking place.

"And now, our final contestant deserves a special word of commendation. Without her assistance this Awards Ceremony would not have been possible."

There was a fanfare of trumpets from the orchestra.

"I give you … Nasti … er … Queen Lilywhite, from the Kingdom of Herenthere!"

The crowd went wild. Everyone thought that Queen Lilywhite had paid for all the splendid decorations and the orchestra and the waiters and the soldiers and the tents and the food and everything, but we know better, don't we? The applause went on and on as Queen Lilywhite, blushing with pleasure, joined the other contestants on the stage.

Then the orchestra played softly as the Lion King came over to shake each contestant by the hand and to thank them for their personal participation in the Great TREK. Then he walked across to the silver perch, put his front paw on the metal bar beside the Owl, crossed his legs and made a short speech. He reminded everyone that the Great TREK had been instituted to celebrate his 40th birthday and in order to advertise the Bushveld to the rest of the World. He thanked all the animals for being such good ambassadors for the Bushveld and told them that he was proud of the way they had behaved towards all the tourists and visitors. He again thanked the four children and their guests for being such wonderful contestants and wished them a safe journey home.

As the King returned to his throne the orchestra started playing and the crowd sang "happy birthday", finishing off with three very loud cheers.

There was another trumpet fanfare from the orchestra and the crowd became silent once more.

In his very important announcer's voice, the Wise Old Owl said, "I now request the King of the Beasts, Louis the Bushveld Lion, to hand over the Awards to our esteemed contestants."

Well, you've all seen awards ceremonies. It would be extremely boring to describe all the "thank you" speeches and hand shaking and applause for every single award, so I'll just tell you who got what and why.

Jak, Kosie, Dorothy and Bobby were each given a bar of gold. This is South Africa's most precious metal and comes from the "heart" of the country ... the mines deep below the African veld. It was a proper and fitting reward for the four South African children who had performed so well for their country.

Humpty-Dumpty was given a lifetime supply of local Zam-Buk ointment (to replace the vinegar and brown paper) for all the bumps and bruises that his shell would take in the years to come. The King's Horse was given a beautiful, wonderfully soft leopard-skin saddle blanket. The King's Man was given a commemorative medal to wear on his uniform.

Bandilegs was given his own magic wand. This was a special wand. The Wise Old Owl had consulted the Tokolossies, and they had designed and ordered the magic wand (from "overseas") themselves. The special feature was that bad spells that he tried to cast on others were all reversed, and would happen to **him** instead. When he got back home, it didn't work. When he opened it up to replace the batteries he found a little label under the flap. It said "Made in China."

Sterling Mustard was given a brand-new GPS, with local maps, so that he would never get lost in South Africa again. When he and Mac drove down to Cape Town to board the ship for the cruise back to the USA, he got lost and landed up on a cattle ranch in Botswana.

Mac was given a vehicle-tracking unit so that he would always know where to find Sterling, no matter where he was in the World. He managed to locate Sterling in Botswana and take him safely back to America.

Yeti and Dodgy were both awarded with a special GREAT TREK Kruger Rand, to make up for the Kruger Millions that they had searched for, but could not find. As a special dispensation, Yeti was given a Royal Bushveld Pardon for all the speeding fines, dust-making fines and destruction-of-property fines that he had accumulated during his visit. He also received a certificate from the van der Merwes of South Africa, in recognition of his contribution to their gainful employment during the year.

For her contribution to the TREK, but more especially for helping the Owl to stage the Awards Ceremony, Queen Lilywhite was given a beautiful blue-white diamond to place in the centre of her crown. She and the Kings and Queens of England would be the only rulers in the World to have a South African diamond in their Crown Jewels. Then, as a special gift from the wine-growers of Stellenbosch, she was also given a box full of South African vine cuttings to plant in her own kingdom when she returned.

As he completed the handing over of the awards, the Lion King made the best award of all. He invited all the contestants to visit South Africa, and especially the Bushveld, whenever they pleased and as often as they liked. The band played and the crowd cheered.

There was a long debate between the contestants before the ceremony to decide who would make a speech on their behalf at the end of the show. It was decided that Dodgy would do the job, as all the others were so self-important that the speech would probably go on for ages.

So, after all the awards were done, Dodgy stepped up to speak. The officer of the guard called all the soldiers to attention and saluted. Like the Lion King, Dodgy stood beside the Wise Old Owl, placed a hoof on the perch and crossed his legs (and did he look cool in his black bow-tie?). An expectant hush fell over the crowd. Dodgy had learned never to clear his throat before speaking as it made the most dreadful sound, so he spoke straight out, from his heart.

"Thanks, Louis," he said. "You're a cool dude."

Dodgy's short speech brought the house, and the curtain, down. There were fireworks and fanfares. The Great TREK was over.

The next day was a rush and bustle of packing and farewells. Eventually the dust settled and the veld returned to normal. Jak sat with his hands behind his head and his back against a *soetdoringboom* (sweet-thorn tree) enjoying the silence. He was also thinking about the events of the past few months. It had been an exciting and wonderful experience, but he was glad that it was over. The visitors were gone, the crowds were gone, the ribbons and banners and flags and musicians and horses and soldiers were gone. All that remained was the wonderful, peaceful Bushveld. As Jak sat watching the glorious sunset, the piercing cry of a fish eagle rang out across the veld. He sighed contentedly.

There's no place like home!

ABOUT THE AUTHOR

Marius Oelschig is a retired soldier, now living in the small Town of Okotoks, in Alberta, Canada ... in the shadow of the Rockies. He only started writing seriously after his grandchildren were born, the first in 2001 – in Canada. When they were old enough, he started writing stories to introduce them to the land of their parents and grandparents, South Africa. As children visiting South Africa, they came to appreciate the veld, the bush, the warm and sunny climate and the open space – pleading for more books about the country they had come to know and love. And so, over the years he has written eight children's books, now available as Kindle e-books and/or as print-on-demand books through Amazon.

Look for his iconic toy soldier at the end of every story and on the back cover of every book

www.ingramcontent.com/pod-product-compliance
Lightning Source LLC
Chambersburg PA
CBHW020249130626
46549CB00005B/2137

* 9 7 8 0 9 9 4 8 4 7 9 5 9 *